Pool Girls

by Cassie Waters

Dive In!

Simon Spotlight
New York   London   Toronto   Sydney   New Delhi

This book is a work of fiction. Any references to historical events, real people, or real locales are used fictitiously. Other names, characters, places, and incidents are the product of the author's imagination, and any resemblance to actual events or locales or persons, living or dead, is entirely coincidental.

SIMON SPOTLIGHT

An imprint of Simon & Schuster Children's Publishing Division

1230 Avenue of the Americas, New York, New York 10020

Copyright © 2012 by Simon & Schuster, Inc.

All rights reserved, including the right of reproduction in whole or in part in any form.

SIMON SPOTLIGHT and colophon are registered trademarks of Simon & Schuster, Inc.

Text by Sarah Albee

For information about special discounts for bulk purchases, please contact Simon & Schuster Special Sales at 1-866-506-1949 or business@simonandschuster.com.

Manufactured in the United States of America 0312 OFF

First Edition 10 9 8 7 6 5 4 3 2 1

ISBN 978-1-4424-4144-6 (pbk)

ISBN 978-1-4424-5375-3 (hc)

ISBN 978-1-4424-4145-3 (eBook)

Library of Congress Catalog Card Number 2011935849

Chapter One

Before she could chicken out, Grace took three quick steps forward and jumped.

Her arms flew over her head as she drove her left knee up. She hit the board, then propelled her body up, up, up into the air. As she bent forward, her hips rose above her head and her arms reached for her toes. For a fraction of a second, her body was completely weightless, high above the water at the top of her dive. Then *whoosh*—she unfolded her legs, straightened her body, and reached for the water that was rushing up to meet her. Down she plunged, deep into the sapphire-blue water. Under here it was another place, a Blue World, muffled, safe, her own private domain.

She swam underwater all the way to the wall. Then she popped to the surface, shook the water from her eyes, and pulled herself out of the pool. She headed over to her chair, where her friend Jaci, wearing huge sunglasses, was reclining and reading a book. Grace glanced down at the book as she grabbed her towel. "You're reading our *Spanish* textbook over Memorial Day *weekend*?"

Jaci shrugged, set down the book, and shimmied up to a sitting position. "We have a vocab quiz tomorrow, remember?"

"Well, I choose to forget, just for a couple of days, how bad I am at Spanish. Every time I ask Ms. Pereira to explain something to me, she answers me in Spanish."

"Yeah, I stink at it, too. That's why I'm brushing up. I really need to improve my grade. Plus I have to get ahead because I have a big clarinet recital coming up."

Grace didn't know Jaci superwell, but in the one class they had together (the first class they'd ever had together), she'd quickly realized that Jaci was "That Person"—the kind that walks out of a test moaning about how she failed it for sure, but then aces it and makes everyone else feel bad about themselves.

"This Thursday I'm allowed to bring a buddy here again," said Jaci. "You want to come with me after school?"

"Sure!" Grace said. Did she sound too eager?

"Do you think your parents will let you join RSC for the summer?" asked Jaci. "I mean, it's nice to have you as my guest, but they only let you do that four times a month. It would be cool if you could become a member. I wouldn't mind hanging out with someone with a brain in her head."

"I'm working on it big-time with my mom and dad," said Grace. "I'm doing my chores before they need doing, cranking out my homework before they start nagging, even practicing piano before they ask."

"They'll cave," said Jaci. "Keep up the pressure."

"It *would* be great to join this place." Grace sat down on the edge of her chair and looked around Riverside Swim Club and its huge, T-shaped swimming pool. The diving boards and platforms were just begging to be used. On the other side was a lane pool, filled with splashing kids in one section and serious lane swimmers in the rest. Around the corner was the little-kid pool.

"It's kind of a scene here, though," Jaci continued. "I thought about joining the girls' swim team, but it looks pretty cliquey. Plus I stink at competitive swimming."

"Me too," said Grace.

"The nice thing is, my mom has a zillion friends who belong, and they all take turns being the 'responsible adult,'" said Jaci, putting air quotes around the last two words. "Middle school kids like us have to be here with an adult, but my mom and her friends let us do our own thing. It's great."

"That *is* great," Grace agreed.

"The boys' team is supercompetitive, but they're all annoying jocks, especially their studly star, Mike Morris. They're all about how they look, strutting around in their jammers."

"Jammers?"

"Those tight swim trunks they wear. Speaking of studly—have you checked out Gorgeous Jordan up there? Drool!" She gestured with her chin toward the lifeguard chair at the far end of the other pool, where Jordan Lee, a high school junior, sat surveying the pool like a god looking down from Mount Olympus.

Grace glanced at him. "He's okay." Then she turned back to the water. "I love the diving boards here. I'm going back in. Want to come?"

"Nah, I'm good. I'll be here, studying my irregular verbs." She grinned at Grace.

"Gee, sounds like a laugh a minute," said Grace. She headed back to the diving board.

Step-step-step–drive the knee–JUMP!

This time she got really high off the board, high enough that she had time to touch her toes, unfold, and stre-e-e-tch her fingers toward the water. *Whoosh!* The bubbles roared in her ears down in the Blue World. She knew it had been a good dive.

As her head emerged from the water, she was startled to see another head not far away from her, near the other springboard. A boy was hanging on to the edge of the pool, wearing tinted goggles, which gave him a froglike look. Where had *he* come from?

"Nice front pike," he called. He had an unexpectedly deep voice, dark brown and velvety.

Grace resisted the urge to dive back down into the Blue World and wait for him to go away. Good thing she was in the cool water, because she felt the usual hot flush rising up to her hairline. "Thanks," she said, and propelled herself to the side of the pool. All she'd done was dive. She had no idea it was called a front spike or whatever he'd said. She pulled herself out of the water and clambered clumsily to her feet, willing herself not to pluck at her wet suit, which was clinging to her in all kinds of embarrassing ways.

The boy swiveled up and out of the pool in one smooth movement, and a moment later was standing a few feet away from her. He pulled up his goggles, drained out the water, and snapped them on top of his head. Then he began flinging excess water off his arms. His hair was slicked-back and smooth like a seal's. He looked about her age, or a year older, and was several inches taller, with powerful shoulder muscles. Grace was tall for her age, and usually towered over boys.

She darted a second glance at him, which was time enough to take in the huge green eyes spiked with long eyelashes. He was take-your-breath-away gorgeous. Her paralyzing shyness flooded in like a wave swirling and eddying around rocks.

"You swim too?" he asked. He didn't even look her way, but now bent over to brush the water off his legs.

"Um. Not actually." Not *actually*? Inward groan. "I stink at swimming." *Great. Tell him all your other faults while you're at it,* she thought. *Maybe you can work in what a disaster you are at Spanish.* She prayed her feet wouldn't spontaneously slip out from under her or something.

The boy straightened up and turned to go. "Well, see ya."

"Um, see ya." She turned her body toward Jaci's chair, but out of the corner of her eye she followed him as he walked away.

"Want to get a snack at the snack bar?" someone next to her said.

Grace jumped—literally—out of her stare.

"I didn't mean to startle you!" the someone continued. It was Jaci.

"Yeah, sure," said Grace, absentmindedly. "So who's that guy over there?" She tried to get her voice back down an octave as she gestured with her chin toward the boy. He had stopped to talk to an older guy with a whistle around his neck.

Jaci snorted. "Oh. *Him. That's* Mike Morris."

Clackety-clack-clack. Grace quickly flicked off the vacuum cleaner. No telling what she'd just vacuumed up from under her bed. Still, it looked pretty good in here. She'd kept her word and had maintained a pretty decent level of cleanliness in her bedroom for at least three weeks now. Not an easy feat considering that she was an artist, and what artist is expected to maintain a tidy painting studio? Still, her art corner looked pretty good. Brushes and pencils in their cups, pastels and charcoals on the shelves, paper stacked in organized piles, the worst paint stains scrubbed out of the carpet.

Last year her mom had helped her put up mounting board along one whole wall of her room and then painted it the same color purple as the walls, so now she could tack anything she wanted on that wall from floor to ceiling. You practically couldn't see the purple anymore, what with the drawings, paintings, posters, and pictures of her favorite musicians, celebrities, and fashion designers that she'd torn out of magazines.

Grace retracted the cord on the vacuum and then fell back onto her bedspread, a riot of funky geometric shapes in different shades of purple, green, and silver. Her back felt pleasantly unpleasant: just a hint of sunburn despite her having slathered herself with sunblock. It felt like summer.

She thought about that boy Mike. Was there such a thing as love at first sight? Those eyes. Those broad shoulders. And he was tall! She didn't think real boys actually looked like that outside the pages of magazines, and without the miracle of Photoshop. But he did exist.

She made herself snap out of it. *Yes, this is definitely a sophisticated teenager kind of bedroom,* she thought as she scanned the crowded wall of images. No one needed to know that she stored her tattered old toddler blanket and stuffed hippo in the cabinet next to her bed. Ages ago, she used to bring that hippo to sleepovers with her best friends, Christina Cooper and Mel Levy. Christina would bring her teddy bear, and Mel her stuffed monkey.

Over to the left, almost behind the door, Grace had tacked up a piece of paper—actually, two pieces, taped together lengthwise—folded like an accordion and filled with scribbled words written with different-colored inks in large, bubbly handwriting. It was a story she and Christina had written together back when they were in second grade, something about a dragon and a princess. Below that she'd tacked up several friendship bracelets she and Christina and Mel had woven at day camp together and that she couldn't quite bring herself to throw away.

Sometimes she really missed those days, when life seemed so much less complicated and when she and Christina and Mel had sworn to one another that they'd be best friends for life. But lately, well . . . things had changed. She lay there contemplating her wall until her mother called her to set the table.

At dinner Grace brought up the most important topic right away. "Soooo, have you guys thought more about it?"

Her father pronged his carbonara and spun it around and around his fork. "Thought about what?"

She sighed. "You know what. About letting me join RSC this summer. Have you noticed how clean I've been keeping my room? And how my Spanish grade went up? Well, a little, anyway."

Her parents exchanged a look. This generally meant they'd already discussed the issue privately and had come up with a joint decision. Her mother set down her glass. "Grace. Honey. We've had a membership at the lake for practically your whole life. Why all of a sudden do you want to up and join a different club? I never knew you to be that interested in joining a swim club."

"That's because I didn't know what I was missing!" said Grace. "It would be really fun to hang out with more kids my own age for a change. The kids at the lake are all little. RSC is awesome, and only a bike ride away. You should see the facilities. They have a three-meter diving board and a diving platform."

Her mother shook her head. "It's too expensive to belong to both places. Remember, we do have your brother's college tuition bills to contend with these days."

Her father looked thoughtful. "You know, Kristin, it could be a nice change for us as a family. I could take up lap swimming in the morning."

Grace had just taken a sip of milk, and it very nearly went down the wrong pipe. "No!" she said after she'd stopped coughing. "I don't mean joining as a *family*! That's . . . that's way too expensive! And you guys love it at the lake! I'd never dream of taking that away from you! I'd just join RSC as an individual member. You just need a parent or designated responsible adult to be there with you—and Jaci's mom and her friends are there all summer long. It's only two hundred dollars if you're under eighteen. I looked into it."

Her father took off his glasses and set them down on the table, then massaged his temples. This was his way of thinking about what he was going to say. *It probably works really well when he is arguing his cases in the courtroom,* Grace thought, not for the first time.

"Okay, missy," he said, looking at her from beneath his dramatically dark eyebrows, which, unfortunately, Grace had inherited. "Here's the deal. Your mother and I are willing to entertain this idea of yours, provided you continue to keep your grades up—"

"Oh, wow! That's awesome!"

"Not so fast. As I was saying, provided you keep your grades up, and"—he paused to put his glasses back on, probably another courtroom mannerism—"you get a job and earn the cost of the membership yourself."

The smile evaporated from Grace's face like a wet

footprint on a hot day. "But how am I supposed to earn two hundred dollars over the next two weeks? By robbing a *bank*?"

Her mother smiled and swiveled Grace's plate around so the carrot sticks were right in front of her. "Let's hope that won't be necessary. Actually, I already have two leads for you. At Ellie's piano lesson this afternoon, Mrs. Orben asked me if I thought you might be interested in babysitting her kids for the next two Saturday nights. She has to take the evening nursing shift at the hospital, and as you know it's Mr. Orben's busy season at the garden store."

Grace nodded thoughtfully. The Orben kids could be a handful, but they were basically good kids. "What's the other job?"

"Dog sitting."

"Please don't tell me for Boomer."

"For Boomer."

Grace groaned and shoved her plate forward so she could lay an anguished cheek down on the table. She looked up and blinked at her mother. "Boomer is the dumbest, most annoying, slobberiest dog I have ever met. He jumps up and tries to knock you over. And if you so much as look at him he drools all over you."

"They're leaving Wednesday for a week of vacation, and Mrs. Barber's father just had shoulder surgery, so Boomer's doggy grandparents can't watch him as they'd planned."

"Did Boomer dislocate his shoulder or something? I wouldn't put it past him. He weighs more than I do." She took a moody bite of carrot, being careful to use her molars due to her braces.

A smile tugged at the corners of her mother's mouth. "No, Grace. Boomer is a sweet dog. And they're willing to pay you eight dollars a day."

This bucked her up. Grace stood up and collected her dirty dishes. "Okay," she said.

"That's the spirit," said her father, standing up to help clear more dishes. "You'll appreciate RSC more if you work for it. And look at your brother—he landed a summer job at that camp."

Grace rolled her eyes. "May I remind you that Cam's in college and I'm just in middle school?"

"So it's settled, then," said her mother. "Now go call the Orbens and the Barbers and get your instructions. And after that—"

"I know, I know. I'll practice, just like I always do with hardly any reminding," said Grace in a singsongy voice.

Her mother shook her head and muttered, "You'd think the daughter of a piano teacher wouldn't ever need *any* reminding."

Grace raced off to make the calls. After she spoke with the Orbens and the Barbers, she texted Mel with the news. She thought about texting Christina as well, but didn't. Christina always spent a big chunk of the summer at a sleep-away camp. But they'd always spent the first three weeks of summer vacation hanging out together. Maybe she'd think that if Grace joined RSC it was Grace's way of saying she didn't want to be such close friends. Grace decided she'd wait to break the news to Christina, in case it didn't actually happen.

Chapter Two

So did you finish *Call of the Wild*?" Grace asked Christina as they stood at their lockers the next morning. "It took me forever."

"Yeah, me too," agreed Christina. "But whatever. Just thirteen more days of school to get through and then it's *summer!*"

"I so cannot wait," said Grace, opening her locker. She thought again about mentioning to Christina her plan to join RSC. But then again, why would Christina even care? She'd be off soon for her fancy camp. Grace was a little sick of hearing about how fabulous it was. Well, when she had enough for her RSC membership, maybe Grace could do a little bragging right back.

"Grace, you know you have to clear that mess out before the end of the year, right?"

Grace felt her face flush. To hide it, she squatted down to search for her grammar workbook at the bottom of her locker, beneath mounds of books and art stuff and shoes. "I think my stuff has undergone mitosis," she muttered. "It's divided and multiplied and regenerated at the bottom of my locker, and I can't find *anything*."

"No offense, but you're such a pack rat," said Christina. "Most of that stuff looks like junk, anyway." She peered into her own neat, decorated, and well-organized locker. She unscrewed a wand of shimmery pink lip gloss and looked in the mirror she'd mounted inside the locker door. Below the mirror, she had taped up pictures of movie actors, tennis stars, and pop singers. She opened her eyes wide and moved her head from side to side as she applied the lip gloss, her glossy brown hair swishing like in a shampoo commercial. Then, apparently satisfied, she put the lip gloss back into her locker and closed the door.

Grace tried not to stare at Christina's hair. It always looked so perfect and never had a hint of frizz, even on a swelteringly humid day like today. Unlike her own reddish-brown mousy hair, which frizzed if she so much as looked outside on a rainy day.

"Hey, you," murmured a low voice on the other side of Christina.

Grace, still kneeling on the floor, leaned back a little so she could peer past Christina and see who it was. Marc LaRocque, the to-die-for star of the hockey team! He was the one recognizable player on the ice, thanks to his long, blond curls, which coiled around his hockey helmet.

"So I was wondering? If you were, um, planning on going to the dance with anyone?"

Grace held her breath, hoping they wouldn't notice she was kneeling right there listening. Marc LaRocque and his blond curls were asking Christina *out*!

Christina furrowed her brow as though a troubled thought had just occurred to her. Then she smiled. "You are so sweet!" she trilled. "But I already said yes to some-one else! Promise me you'll ask me to dance, though? Pretty please?"

Grace couldn't swear to it, because Christina was mostly in profile, but it certainly seemed as though Christina batted her heavily mascaraed eyelashes at the guy. Still kneeling on the floor, Grace rolled her eyes.

Marc shrugged. "Sure, yeah. Got to get to class." He bolted away down the hall, where he soon vanished into the stream of kids hurrying to class.

Grace finally spotted her book and tugged it out of the other junk. A big corner of the back cover was bent down, but at least she had it. She stood up and faced Christina.

"Are you really going with someone else?"

Christina giggled conspiratorially. "Well, not exactly. But I need to keep my options open. He's pretty hot, though, isn't he?"

Grace's jaw dropped. "Yeah!" she said. "I can't believe you turned him down!"

Christina's eyes flickered from Grace's face down to her functional-but-unfashionable T-shirt, jeans, and flip-flops, then back up to her face. "Have you ever thought about straightening your hair?"

"No." Grace's eyes narrowed. "So you think if I just straightened my hair and wore makeup someone would ask me to the dance?"

"I did *not* say that!" Christina retorted. Then she heaved a sigh and turned squarely to face Grace. "Listen. A couple of us are going to the mall this Saturday to pick up some last-minute stuff for the dance, maybe get mani-pedis, that kind of thing. You want to come?"

"Uh, sure. If it's not too late in the afternoon. I have to babysit Saturday night. Who's going?"

"Just me, and, well, Lindsay and Ashley. And possibly Veronica Massey."

Lindsay Petrarca? Ashley Karcher? Veronica Massey? So they were more than just school friends, Grace confirmed to herself. When she thought about it, she had noticed Christina hanging around those girls the past few weeks. She didn't know Veronica very well, but just at the beginning of this school year, she and Christina and Mel had declared Lindsay and Ashley tied for first place on their list of World's Most Annoying People. Was she serious? But all Grace said was, "Okay, yeah. Can I invite Mel, too?"

Christina hesitated. "Do you think she'll feel comfortable around those girls? She seems so . . . critical these days."

"Mel? Critical? What of?"

Christina shrugged. "Never mind. Anyway, sure she can come. Although my mom will probably drive us in the little car, so maybe you guys should just meet us there? At like, one, at the fountain?"

The bell rang. Grace closed her locker. "Sounds good," she said over her shoulder as she followed the last stragglers hurrying off to homeroom.

English class with Mr. Cayer was just before lunch. Grace's stomach was already growling and there were fifty-five minutes to get through before the bell rang. The windows in the classroom were open, and the air was warm and thick with the promise of summertime.

Mr. Cayer, wearing an unfashionable tie and slightly rumpled shirt, paced between the rows of desks, his hands in his pockets jingling his change, waiting for kids to come in and settle down. Most kids thought he was a hard grader, but Grace liked him. He told amusing stories about his artist wife and his infant daughter, and how he spent his summers working on a novel, a murder mystery featuring a hard-boiled detective.

Christina sat next to Grace on one side, while Veronica Massey sat on the other. Rashid Stokes, the class clown, sat a couple of desks behind Grace and could be depended on to crack up the class at least once a period.

"I know summer is only a few weeks away, but I hope you all finished *Call of the Wild* this weekend, because it's time for a reading check," said Mr. Cayer, which was met with a chorus of groans from the class. "Reading check" was code for a pop quiz. "Take out a piece of paper and answer the following question. Give me three paragraphs with good lead sentences." He hit a button on his laptop and the question appeared on the whiteboard.

"And so it went, the inexorable elimination of the super-fluous." What does London mean by this sentence? You may use your books to find examples to back up your assertions.

For the next twenty minutes all was quiet except for the scribbling of pencils and shuffling of book pages. A couple of times Grace's mind drifted to images of the glittery pool and a smiling Mike Morris, but she managed to snap back to the question in front of her. When Grace finally finished, she put her pencil down, stretched out her fingers, and sighed. Summer couldn't come fast enough.

Mr. Cayer collected the essays and returned to the front of the room. Without looking in Christina's direction, he cleared his throat and said, "Miss Cooper. Unless that smartphone is the Oracle telling you the Meaning of Life, and you'd like to share that knowledge with the rest of us, please cease texting under your desk and surrender your phone to me."

Christina groaned. Busted. Slowly she extended her arm and held out her phone for Mr. Cayer to collect, looking like a queen waiting for her servant to take off her glove for her. Mr. Cayer took the phone and flipped it into the air and caught it, then placed it on his desk.

"We'll talk later. I ought to turn it in to Mrs. MacMullen and have her call your parents, as this is a repeat offense. But let's see if we can find another *Call of the Wild* question for you to answer instead."

Christina beamed at Mr. Cayer. "Sounds like a deal. Thanks, Mr. C. Detention is really overrated, isn't it? I mean, why waste my youth?"

Mr. Cayer's mouth twitched. "Come see me during eighth period study hall," he said, and moved on with the lesson. *Amazing*, Grace thought. Any other student and Mr. Cayer would have sent her straight to the principal for a guaranteed detention. But, as Grace's father had once put it, Christina could charm the skin off a snake.

"Maybe if you did a little more *reading* of the text and a little less *sending* of texts, you'd discover you have a lot to contribute to our discussions," said Mr. Cayer with a wry half smile on his face. He turned and wrote a quotation on the board: *"A dog could break its heart through being denied the work that killed it."* He turned back to the class. "Who can tell me what this statement means?"

"He's talking about Spitz," Grace muttered under her breath. "Spitz is sick but he wants to be part of the team." But Grace wasn't about to raise her hand. Too many strong personalities in this class. She wished she weren't such a wuss about speaking in front of other people. Another thing to work on this summer.

Veronica Massey's hand shot up. *How does she manage to be smart and popular?* Grace wondered, not for the first time. "He's talking about Spitz, the dog," she said. "Spitz is too sick to keep up with the dog team, but it's the only thing he wants to do so he dies of a broken heart."

"Good," said Mr. Cayer.

Grace inwardly groaned. *Why couldn't I just raise my hand and say that?* she thought.

The class droned on until at long last the bell rang. Grace shot up from her seat as though someone had hit the eject button. Luckily the classroom was close to the cafeteria, so she could get there before the line got too long. "Boy, that was a close call with your phone, huh?" she said to Christina.

Christina grimaced. "And it figures I would get in trouble texting my *mom*. Not even a friend, which might have been worth it." She shook her head. "There is just way too much drama in my home life right now."

Grace waited for Christina to share more information, but she didn't seem to want to talk about it. "Coming to lunch?" Grace asked as she zipped up her backpack and slung it onto one shoulder.

"You go ahead," said Christina. "I'm—ah—supposed to meet Lindsay outside her class."

Grace drooped. "Okay. See you there," she said, and hurried out into the river of chattering students.

Why was Christina always with Lindsay or Ashley these days? It's true she and Grace had been growing apart the past few months, but they *always* walked to lunch together.

Luckily, Mel fell into step with her just as she got to the door of the cafeteria. "Smells like fish sticks," she said, sniffing the air. "Again."

"Christina invited us to go to the mall with her on Saturday," said Grace. She didn't mention that she'd had to ask Christina to include Mel, of course.

Mel curled her lip. "I'll think about it," she said. "Christina's been pretty snotty to me this whole year."

"Look," Grace said, nudging Mel. "There's Marc LaRocque. He asked Christina to the dance."

Mel swiveled her head to look in a way that was not at all subtle and made Grace cringe. Marc was sitting with Max Mosello and Alex Hernandez. The three hottest guys in the school all around one table.

"Stop staring," Grace hissed as they collected their trays and pushed them down the food line.

"Christina is sitting with Lindsay and Ashley yet again," said Mel. "What a shocker."

Grace shrugged. "She's in the popular crowd now, it seems. Come on. I see Emily and Jaci waving us over. Let's sit with them."

Social studies was right after lunch, which sometimes made it hard to stay alert. But Ms. Holmes had arranged the desks in a big oval, which meant you couldn't get droopy-eyed or everyone would notice. Grace and Mel always sat next to each other, opposite Lindsay and Ashley.

"So did I tell you the new plan for the summer?" asked Mel as they walked into the classroom. "We're going to be away for ten weeks. My dad got a really good rental deal for a house at the shore."

Grace stopped dead at this news, which caused Chris Capece to crash into her from behind.

"Uh, Grace? You want to not stop like that?" he said, stooping to pick up the notebook and pencil case he'd dropped.

"Sorry, sorry," mumbled Grace as she managed to collect herself enough to drift into the classroom.

"Grace, I told you I was going away this summer," Mel

reminded her, swinging into her seat and propping her chin on her hand.

"Yeah, but you didn't say you'd be gone for ten whole weeks," said Grace. She dropped her backpack to the floor and sat down heavily. "What am I going to do without you all summer?"

"I thought you were going to join RSC," said Mel. "You'll have a blast there."

Grace groaned. "If I ever manage to raise the money. Otherwise it's going to be fun-time summer at the lake, getting sand dumped on me by toddlers in swim diapers and arm floaties."

Chapter Three

Wednesday morning. Grace opened one eye and checked the clock: five minutes to six, and five minutes until the alarm was going to ring. Then she heard the rain pattering on the roof. She groaned and rolled the pillow around her ears, snuggling deeper under the covers. Of all the days for it to pour, why did it have to be on her first day of dog sitting? But then again, eight dollars a day was eight dollars a day. She rolled over and clicked off the alarm, then sat up in bed, her eyes still closed, trying to adjust to the awake state. Mornings were not her best time of the day. She got out of bed, pulled on yesterday's jeans and a sweatshirt from off the floor, and practically sleepwalked out of her room.

"Hello, Boomer, you big, slobbery canine," she mumbled a few minutes later as she opened the Barbers' back door with the key they'd left for her. She pushed inside. Boomer bounded over to her as though she were a long-lost best friend. His huge paws with their thick black toenails clitter-clattered as he jumped around, his tail wagging so wildly she was afraid it would knock over a kitchen chair.

"No jumping. No *jumping*!" He jumped up on her any-way. "Ugh, this dog," she muttered. She pulled down the dripping hood of her raincoat and reached out gingerly to pat him on the head, but he somehow managed to swivel around to lick her fingers and she got a handful of slob-ber for her efforts. "Eww," she said, wiping her hand on her damp pant leg. This was going to be a long week. She scanned the note Mrs. Barber had left for her, then located the food bin, put two scoops of food in his bowl, and refilled his water dish. He galumphed over to his dish and began devouring the food with loud crunching noises. He'd nearly finished what she'd put in the bowl by the time she found the leash and the scooper. "All right, drool-machine, let's go for a walk," she said, clicking the leash to his collar. And out they went into the pouring rain.

The walk took longer than she'd anticipated, and Grace had to spend time blow-drying her sopping hair, so she missed the bus. Luckily her dad had to get to work early, which meant she could catch a ride with him.

"Tomorrow you'll have to get up earlier," he said, turning the volume down on the car radio.

"Yeah, or take Boomer for a shorter walk," agreed Grace, trying to comb her still-damp, unruly hair with her fingers. Oh, what was the point? Her hair was a failure today no matter what. *Christina will be sure to point that out,* she thought sadly. The rain had stopped, but a light mist had replaced it, the kind that comes up under your umbrella and is guaranteed to frizz your hair to maximum capacity. "Do you mind dropping me off just after the stop sign? It's kind of crowded this time of the morning and I don't want you to get blocked in or anything."

Her dad looked puzzled. "Suit yourself, but it's getting a little late." He shrugged and pulled over.

She didn't have the heart to tell him the real reason. Why would a grown man think he looked good in that ratty, old baseball hat he had on? Maybe because it covered his thinning hair, so he thought he looked younger? Her father loved that hat. It was fine around the house, but she wasn't about to be seen getting out of a car driven by a dad in a midlife crisis. Really, for a dad he could be awfully immature sometimes.

They pulled up behind a fancy car and Grace saw Jaci get out and slam the door. "Thanks, gotta go!" Grace said. She hurried to catch up with Jaci, her backpack bouncing on her shoulders with every step.

"As usual, my mom couldn't find her car keys this morning," grumbled Jaci. "Just once it would be nice to get to school on time."

The first bell had already rung, so both girls hustled off to their lockers.

In homeroom, announcements had begun when Grace slid breathlessly into her seat.

". . . *reminder that the end-of-the-year dance is just one week from this Friday. Please sign up at the dance committee table at lunchtime if you haven't yet done so.*"

"Hey," said a voice behind her. She felt a poke in the ribs and turned around. It was Veronica Massey. "Are you going?"

Grace gaped at her. What did Veronica Massey care if she, Grace Davis, was going to the dinner-dance?

"I'm on the dance committee, and I was going through the lists and didn't see your name. We're going for maximum participation. Plus we're selling raffle tickets."

Oh, well, that explained it. Grace nodded. "Yeah, I think I am. I'll bring in money tomorrow. Then I have to fly to Paris for the weekend and pick up my dress." Ha-ha. She was such a riot. Why did she have to keep talking? Obviously Veronica would think her attempt at a joke was lame. Clearly, what to wear was not an issue for Veronica Massey, who never seemed to appear in the same outfit twice. She probably *did* fly to Paris to buy her dresses.

Veronica smiled. For a popular girl, she had a nice smile, Grace was surprised to see. "I'm sure you'll look great," she said, and leaned back toward her own desk.

Grace did have a dress, sort of. A few weeks ago her aunt Beth had sent a big box of clothes from her teenage daughter—Grace's cousin Candace. "Cand-me-downs," as Grace called them. Included in the carton had been a semi-fancy dress. But Candace was petite and well-developed in all the right places. Grace, on the other hand, was tall and skinny and all elbows and knees. "A human carpenter ruler," her brother, Cameron, had so charmingly described her. The dress was too short and definitely too roomy in the bust.

~~~~~

"*Please, please, please* come to the mall on Saturday?" Grace begged Mel as they headed to social studies. "Say yes, and then I'll tell you who's coming."

Mel peered at her suspiciously through her fashionably dorky, black-framed glasses. "Who's going to be there?"

"Say yes."

Mel sighed. "Okay, yes. My mom wanted to take me anyway because I need a new pair of sandals. Now, who's going to be there?"

"Well, I told Christina I'd meet her there. She's going with Lindsay and Ashley. And maybe Veronica. But we have to get our own ride because there's no room in their car."

Mel pursed her lips thoughtfully. "I bet you anything Christina's mom made her invite us. Clearly this was an existing plan and we're an afterthought."

Grace, of course, knew that Mel hadn't been part of the original plan. But it was a shock to think she, too, hadn't been included. Was Mel right?

Mel blew a strand of hair away from her face. "Okay, I'll come. I'll ask my mom to drive us, and you can help me find some sandals."

"Deal," Grace said, relieved.

"Your final projects on Asia are due a week from today—next Wednesday," Ms. Holmes announced. "And remember, these must be done in groups of three. Luckily there are twenty-seven of you, so the groupings should come out even. Each group will pick a country out of this basket, and a theme out of this one." She held up a small basket in each hand. "Okay, break into threes."

Grace and Mel immediately scooched their chairs together. "We need one more," said Grace.

"Grace! Pleeeeeease?"

Grace almost fell out of her chair. Lindsay and Ashley were waving her over. They wanted her to be in their group? "Um, sorry, but I'm with Mel," said Grace.

There was a loud *kathunk*ing sound. Grace watched Rashid bump his chair across the floor until he came to a stop on the other side of Mel. He grinned widely at Mel and clasped his hands imploringly. "Mel! Chris and I need someone with a higher-than-average IQ! Be in our group?"

Mel and Grace exchanged a look. Then Mel shook her head. "Sorry, Rashid. I'm with Grace."

Grace turned to Ashley and Lindsay. Her mouth went dry and she swallowed twice. Why was she so intimidated by them? Then she stammered out, "W-why doesn't one of you join our group and one of you go with Rashid and Chris?"

Ashley looked at Chris and Rashid like she'd just sniffed a carton of milk that had turned sour. "Here's a better idea," she said to Grace. "You be with us, and she can go with them."

Grace nodded quickly. She nearly always caved when going up against a bossy person. She looked at Mel with a helpless shrug. "Ummmm, okay," she said slowly. Mel gave her a reproachful look. Deep down, Grace was flattered to be asked by Ashley and Lindsay. Maybe Christina wasn't the only one who might be joining the cool crowd.

Rashid pumped the air with his fist. "You won't regret this, Mel. Our project's going to *rock the house!*"

Mel rolled her eyes, but Grace noted with relief that she didn't look too upset about working with Chris and Rashid.

Grace, Ashley, and Lindsay picked Tibet. Their theme was the arts. Grace breathed a sigh of relief. "We're pretty lucky. We could have chosen some weird theme like the economy, or a hard-to-research country like North Korea," she said.

Lindsay frowned. "No we couldn't. We're studying *Asia.*"

Grace arranged her face in a neutral expression. Was she kidding? Or did she not know that North Korea *was* in Asia? They'd just had a quiz on all the countries of Asia.

"So, Grace. Take over here. What do we do?" said Ashley. She capped a yawn.

Grace felt her face flush. Why did she have to get so tongue-tied? A good idea had just occurred to her, but she just couldn't make herself sound normal and casual sometimes. "Well, um. You guys might have a better idea. But one thing I was thinking was, um, we could make a mandala?"

"A mandah-*what*?" said Lindsay, furrowing her smooth brow. "That sounds like a musical instrument. I can't read music."

"No, actually, it's a sand design that the Buddhist monks create. Remember we saw one in that film last week? We can use colored craft sand and follow a pattern." She braced herself for the girls to say it was a stupid idea.

Lindsay shrugged. "Whatever. Sounds good. You're an artsy type, right? That's what Christina told us."

Christina had told them about her? Grace swelled with gratitude. Maybe Christina was trying, in her own way, to help Grace be popular. Maybe she was going to bring her old friends, Grace and Mel, along with her to the popular crowd. She waited for Lindsay and Ashley to propose a plan, but they just sat there. Lindsay was coiling her long blond hair around her finger. Ashley was doodling on the cover of Grace's notebook. They heard a burst of laughter from Mel's group on the other side of the room. Grace screwed up her courage and just blurted it out. "So do you want to come over to my house this weekend and work on it?"

"We're going to the mall on Saturday," said Ashley. "Christina invited you, too, right?"

"Yeah," said Grace quickly, suddenly even more elated. Looked like Christina really did want to include her in her new group.

"Yeah, but we better figure something out," Lindsay said to Ashley. "Remember the concert is next Tuesday."

"Concert?" asked Grace, deflating a bit.

Ashley and Lindsay exchanged a look. "Nothing," said Ashley. "Sunday sounds like a good time to get together."

"Okay. Sunday, then," said Grace. Was she being too pushy? Neither of them seemed all that interested. And what was this concert? Was Christina going too? If so, why hadn't she mentioned anything about it?

"Cool," said Ashley. "We'll come to your house around four. I'm supposed to have dinner with my dad and step-mom Sunday night, so I'll have them pick me up at your house at, like, five thirty. And we can drop you at home, Linz."

Grace started to say that wouldn't be enough time to get the project finished, but stopped herself. Maybe it would be fine.

She avoided looking across the room at Mel, who was chattering away with Rashid and Chris. She thought she could sense reproachful vibes from Mel rippling across the room, but she chose to pretend they weren't there.

Chapter Four

On Thursday morning, Grace awoke to the patter of raindrops outside and groaned. Still raining. Not only would she have to walk Boomer in the rain once again, but she was also supposed to go back to RSC with Jaci that afternoon. She'd been fantasizing for days about running into Mike there. She decided to pack her suit and towel anyway.

By afternoon the skies had cleared and the rain had stopped. A weak sun tried to push through the clouds. "You still want to go to the club?" Jaci whispered to Grace during Spanish class.

Grace nodded definitively.

Jaci grinned. "Okay. My mom's out of town today, so

we'll have to take the school bus, but it goes right by there. And my mom has a friend who said she'd be our responsible adult."

It was still overcast, so there were few people at the pool that afternoon. But the air was warm and the pool beckoned invitingly. Grace scanned the pool deck for Mike, but without much hope. What were the odds he'd be here on a random Thursday afternoon, and a cloudy one at that? Still, even without a Mike sighting, it was great to be back at RSC. As Jaci settled into a chair to read a book, Grace lowered herself into the water. It felt heavenly. She dove down, then swam as far as she could underwater, loving the muffled, blue-gray stillness below the surface. She stayed in the water until her fingers were wrinkled and her eyes were stinging, and she would have stayed even longer except that Jaci made her come out, complaining she was starving and had to go home and practice her clarinet.

Friday came and went without much incident. Grace continued to walk Boomer. The Barbers were due back the following Wednesday night. Walking Boomer would add sixty-four dollars toward her RSC fund. Added to the thirty-seven she already had stashed in the shoe box in her closet, that meant that she would soon have $101. Just ninety-nine more to go.

On Saturday, just after lunch, Mrs. Levy and Mel picked her up and drove her to the mall. Was Mel upset with her? Grace couldn't really tell. Maybe not. From the front seat, Mel prattled away about the project she was working on with Chris and Rashid.

"Our country is Japan and our theme is food. What could be better? We're going to make sushi, but all three of us are skeeved out by raw fish, so we're going to use tuna from a can. Rashid's dad is a great cook, and they have this huge kitchen and this cool sushi-roller thingie, so we're going to go to his house superearly Wednesday morning and make it there, and Chris's mom is a graphic designer and she has all this cool calligraphy stuff, so she's going to lend it to us and we're going to make the most amazing display boards!"

Grace felt a pang of envy. It sounded like a really fun project, and all three group members seemed to be involved. "My group is getting together tomorrow," said

Grace, trying to sound more bright and upbeat than she felt. "I've been researching how to make a mandala."

"Oh, yeah, that thing we saw in the video?"

"Yep. I found a lot of videos online that show you how."

"So what are Lindsay and Ashley doing?"

Grace hesitated. "They're going to help make it."

Mel looked out the window, and they rode in silence for a moment. "I bet they're psyched to have you as a partner because you're such a good artist."

Grace opened her mouth to say something, then closed it again. *That's probably true,* she thought. "But I can't talk in front of people," she said. "I get so nervous."

"Well, let them do the presenting, then," Mel said simply. "Everyone knows *they're* not shy."

"Have you mentioned Tuesday to Grace yet, Mel?" Mrs. Levy asked.

Mel smacked herself on the forehead. "Forgot. Can you come out to dinner with us for my early birthday? My grandmother's coming to town and she's taking us to Amazon Adventure since I'll be at the shore for my real birthday."

Relief flooded through Grace. Mel wasn't mad! "Yeah! Sounds great! All I have to do is walk Boomer after school, and then I'll be available!"

"Great," said Mel. "I also invited Christina for old time's sake, but she's got some mysterious plans."

The concert, thought Grace.

"Why don't we say six o'clock on Tuesday," Mrs. Levy said as she pulled up in front of the mall entrance. "Have fun, girls," she said as they got out of the car.

"We're meeting them at the fountain," said Grace as she and Mel made their way through the mall to the fountain near the food court. No one was there when they arrived, though. She checked her phone for texts, but there was nothing from Christina. "Hmm. Well, we're only five minutes late," she said uncertainly. But secretly she wondered— had the girls decided to ditch her and Mel?

Mel sat down on a bench and tossed a nickel into the water. She handed another nickel to Grace. Grace tossed it in, then scanned the whole area for Christina. Her gaze moved past a boy in a red T-shirt and surfer trunks with his back toward them, not far away from their bench. Grace stopped and zoomed back. She'd seen this boy before. But where?

He was standing in front of a sports store, texting someone. Broad shoulders, impossibly muscular arms for someone clearly in the middle of his growth spurt, short, spiky brown hair. The boy looked up from his phone, then turned around. Their eyes locked. Grace felt like someone had just twanged her whole self with a gigantic, cosmic rubber band. Then she felt that familiar hot flush crawl up her chest and neck and up to her hairline. Of course she must have been blushing red as a beet. Was she the only person on the face of the earth who blushed this much? Where had she seen those huge green eyes, ringed with ridiculously long lashes for a guy?

It hit her like a thunderbolt. It was Mike Morris. He looked different not dripping wet. But every bit as gorgeous.

Mike seemed to be having trouble placing her, too. His brow clouded, as though he was trying to remember where he'd seen her before. With a little half smile and an upward jerk of his chin, he acknowledged that he at least recognized her, then turned back to his phone again and began texting away.

Grace felt like all her bones had turned to rubber. Had it only been this past Monday that they'd seen each other? Her mind flashed to an image of him standing poolside, swishing off the water from his muscular forearms. Maybe it would suddenly hit him, too, where he'd seen her before.

Maybe any second now he'd look up, smile at her, and stride over and start talking.

"Um, Grace?" Mel began, nudging her arm. "Why are you sitting there opening and closing your mouth like a goldfish? And your face and neck have gone all mottled and blotchy. Say something. Anything. I want to make sure you're not having an allergic reaction or something."

Grace shook herself out of her reverie. Mike was walking purposefully away, as though he were meeting someone. Probably his girlfriend.

"No, I'm fine," said Grace. "I just . . . thought I recognized someone."

Love at first sight most definitely did exist, because love at *second* sight felt almost exactly the same as the first time around.

Mel followed Grace's gaze and saw Mike's retreating figure as he weaved through groups of chattering teenagers and moms pushing strollers. "Whoa. You know that guy? Is he a rock star?"

"I just met him once; that's all," said Grace with a shrug. She checked her phone again. No message from Christina.

"Why don't you text her?" Mel suggested evenly.

"Right. Will do."

SUP? WRU?

A moment later her phone beeped.

SRY. Stuck @ makeup store. Meet here?

Grace typed back:

BRT. CU soon.

"They're at the makeup store. They want us to meet them there."

Mel made a face. "Nice of them to let us know. Whatever. Let's go."

Grace kept looking for Mike the whole way to the store, but he was nowhere to be found.

"You look awesome!" Ashley squealed to Christina as Grace and Mel approached the girls. "Max is going to *die* when he picks you up for the dance."

Christina was sitting on a high, swively stool, her hair clamped back and her face turned upward, while a young woman dressed like a scientist painted sparkly pink stuff on Christina's lips with a tiny brush. *So, Christina is going to the dance with Max,* Grace thought. It wasn't fair. Did every cute guy at Lincoln Middle School have a crush on Christina? Grace noticed that Lindsay, Ashley, and Veronica had had their makeup done too. And also their nails. Hadn't Christina said they might *all* get mani-pedis? *Obviously they've been at the mall for some time already,* Grace thought bitterly.

The woman stepped back to study Christina's face, and Christina smiled at Grace and Mel. "Awesome, isn't it? I'm buying, like, every one of these products so I can look like this at the dance!"

"Would one of you girls like to be next?" said the woman with a smile. Grace was fascinated by her eyelids, which seemed to have been painted with about eleven different shades of blue and gray, and which, she had to admit, really made the woman's blue eyes look incredible.

"I'm good," said Mel quickly.

"Yeah, me too," said Grace. "I can't stand mascara. It just makes me want to rub my eyes. And when I wear lipstick, I look like a little kid that just ate a Popsicle. Anyway, whatever shade of lipstick I wear doesn't seem to go with my green braces." Grace smiled at the woman so she could get a good look at her braces. Then she immediately regretted what she'd said. The others must have thought she was a total dork.

Mel smiled too, but no one else did. The woman frowned at Grace. "You have beautiful, big, brown eyes, sweetie. A little concealer and some shading on the outer corners could really make them pop."

Please, someone, change the subject, Grace thought desperately. The last thing she wanted to do was smear gunk on her face, which was already on the oily side and was a bad case of acne just waiting to happen. She thought back to when she, Mel, and Christina had had a dress-up tea party, back when they were in kindergarten together. They'd worn fancy dress-up clothes and borrowed lipstick and eye shadow from Mel's older sister. But that was dress-up. Why did Grace feel like the last one to grow up?

"She's fine," said Christina, jumping quickly off the stool. "Let's just say she's not the makeup-wearing type. Right, Brace-Face-Grace?"

Veronica had moved away to look at a display of nail polishes, but Ashley and Lindsay both giggled. Grace didn't see what was funny at all. But she laughed wanly, just so the others would know she wasn't offended, even though she was. Anyway, who had the money for this junk? She was saving every penny for her RSC membership.

After the four girls had bought their products, the six of them wandered out of the store, with Grace and Mel slightly behind the other four. As they strolled through the mall, Grace kept darting glances at Christina, Lindsay, Veronica, and Ashley. She had to admit, they all looked pretty amazing.

"Hot guy, eleven o'clock!" hissed Christina.

Six pairs of eyes looked over at the boy walking into the music store ahead of them. It was Mike Morris. Grace's stomach dropped like she was in a runaway elevator.

"OMG," gushed Ashley. "That is Mike Morris! He goes to Shipton Academy and is, like, the hottest guy on the face of the planet."

"He's an awesome swimmer," added Veronica. "He swims at my pool."

"What pool?" asked Christina, her eyes still glued to Mike.

"Riverside Swim Club," said Veronica.

So Veronica was a member at RSC, Grace noted. She was glad Mike hadn't seen them. She felt storklike and dorky-looking, like one of those "fashion don't" pictures in the magazines, especially standing alongside Christina, Veronica, Ashley, and Lindsay, all of whom were wearing the latest trendy clothes. Even Mel looked cool, with her funky glasses, perfect hair that pouffed in just the right way, and petite little gymnast's body.

Christina turned to Grace and Mel. "We're going to

catch a movie at five," she said. "You guys want to come with us?"

Grace felt herself tense. Christina knew perfectly well that Grace had to babysit. Had Christina forgotten, or was she just rubbing it in that they were all staying and having fun without her and Mel?

Mel shook her head. "Can't. My grandmother's flight is coming in this afternoon and I have to be home for dinner."

Grace mumbled something about having to babysit. Was she the only one in the world who had to earn money? It was so unfair. Her parents were always trying to teach her dumb life lessons and made everything harder than it had to be.

"Aw, that's too bad," said Christina, who didn't sound the least bit upset about their not coming along. "Well, we'll let you know if whatever we see is worth seeing, anyway."

Grace had been trying to figure out how to say something to Lindsay and Ashley. She finally just said it. "Do you guys want to come with me to the craft store? So we can get stuff for the project?"

"Nah," said Ashley.

"We trust you," said Lindsay.

"I'm totally clueless about art stuff," added Ashley.

Grace swallowed. "Well, I should peel off and go, then. My dad's coming to get us in a little while." She waited, hoping it would occur to them to chip in some money for the supplies, but they didn't offer. Why couldn't she just work up the nerve to ask them straight-out for the money? She couldn't. It would just be *waaaay* too embarrassing.

"I'll come with you," Mel said quickly. "I have to buy some markers and then we have to look for sandals for me, remember?"

Grace nodded, feeling vaguely miserable. Suddenly she felt someone touch her on the shoulder. She turned around and found herself staring straight up into the beaming face of Mike Morris.

"Hey! I just figured it out! You're the girl I met at the pool, aren't you? I'm Mike."

The air suddenly felt electrically charged, like those pictures in her science textbook showing electrons zooming around a nucleus. Grace could feel the other girls' astonishment. Her face got hot and was probably bright red. All she could do was nod.

"This is the part where you tell me what *your* name is," said Mike with a sideways grin.

Grace couldn't remember anything, let alone her own

name. Suddenly it came to her. "Grace. I'm Grace."

"Oh, okay, Grace. And these must be your friends. Hi. So, well, bye. Maybe I'll see you at the pool again."

"I'm working on it!" Grace blurted out, then instantly regretted it. It was too late to explain that she meant she was working on earning the money, not working on seeing *him* again. Even though she actually was. *Great. Now he thinks I'm a stalker,* she thought.

He turned and walked away. The six girls stared at him as he headed off. He had an athletic walk, one foot turned in slightly. There was a stunned silence. Finally, Christina broke it.

"Oh. My. Gosh. You know him?"

"No. Well, yes. Sort of."

Veronica seemed amused. Ashley's mouth was hanging open in astonishment. Lindsay's perfectly plucked eyebrows were raised. Even Mel's eyes were open so wide they looked unnaturally huge, magnified behind her glasses. Christina just looked irritated.

"Well, I guess you guys better be going," Christina said.

Whatever tiny iota of pride Grace had felt at being approached by Mike Morris vanished. Why was Christina acting so *mad* at her? Was it her fault she knew a hot guy who Christina didn't? She turned to Ashley and Lindsay.

"Okay, so I'll see you guys tomorrow," she said.

"Tomorrow?" asked Lindsay. "Why?"

Ashley nudged Lindsay. "Right, for the project. We'll see you tomorrow."

Lindsay nodded, clearly remembering. They all said good-bye. Grace couldn't help but watch as Christina walked away with Lindsay, Ashley, and Veronica, her head bowed in a whisper, giggling and telling them some secret.

Grace was relieved that only Mel was there to witness her dad pull up in front of the mall. Their minivan had been mortifying enough when it was new, and now it was all battered up. And also, he was wearing his dumb baseball cap.

Grace's dad frowned as he stared into his hand at the change Grace had given him from the craft store. They'd just dropped off Mel and were still in her driveway. "That's it?" he said.

"I had to get a bunch of stuff for the mandala," Grace confessed. "I'm sure Ashley and Lindsay will chip in when they come tomorrow."

Grace's dad grumbled something and drove off.

Grace arrived at the Orbens' promptly at five thirty that evening. She heard the dog barking before Mrs. Orben had even opened the door. When it swung open, Rosie, a black poodle, became an excited, tail-wagging tornado, whirling around between Mrs. Orben and Grace as though she couldn't believe her good fortune. *At least she didn't jump up like Boomer,* Grace thought. Mrs. Orben was dressed in her hospital clothes, with two bobby pins in her mouth and fourteen-month-old Robby in her arms. Robby was wailing. His face was bright red and his nose was running through both nostrils all the way down to his lip. She could see six-year-old Ellie and four-year-old Matt through the doorway into the living room, where they were climbing around on the couch.

"Oh, thank goodness," said Mrs. Orben, although with the bobby pins it came out all garbled. She thrust Robby toward Grace, who automatically held out her arms for the kid. Grace stepped inside holding the sobbing child as Mrs. Orben pulled the pins out of her mouth and raced to the hall mirror, where she jabbed them into her hair. "I'm so sorry to do this to you, Grace!" she shouted over the squalling. "He can't find his weesie and I just don't have time to search for it."

"His what? Weesie?"

"Sorry, his binky. His pacifier. We have others, of course, but this one's his favorite. I'm sure it's somewhere. Ellie and Matthew can help you find it." She looked at herself in the mirror, shrugged, and sat down to lace up her thick-soled white nursing shoes. "Dinner's on the counter; they can have milk or water but don't let them talk you into giving them juice. I guess you can skip baths even though they're pretty filthy from the gymnastics party they went to today. I left a note with bedtimes and what they can watch while you get Robby down. Mr. Orben will be home at nine, on pain of death. Oh, and I forgot to feed Rosie. Ellie can show you where the dog food is."

Grace nodded and shifted the kid from one hip to the other, which wasn't easy, as he'd buried his chubby fists into her hair and had it all twined around them.

"That reminds me!" Mrs. Orben picked up her pocketbook and keys. "Your mother tells me you're a dog sitter. Our neighbors, the Palmers, need a dog sitter next week. They'll be gone Wednesday through Sunday and can pay you fifty dollars. Does that sound like something you might want to do?"

Fifty more dollars! "Yes, sure!" said Grace.

"Great. I don't suppose you're available next Friday night, by chance, are you? Mr. Orben has a business dinner to go to and I have to work again."

"Sorry," said Grace. "That's the night of our end-of-year dance."

"Oh, of course," said Mrs. Orben. "Your mother mentioned it at Ellie's lesson. I should have remembered! Well, I'll see you next Saturday, in any case." Mrs. Orben gave the squalling baby a kiss on the top of his head, deftly side-swiped his attempt to grab her with both of his chubby, outstretched hands, waved to the two older kids in the other room, and opened the door. "Thanks so much, Grace. This is such a big help," she said as she closed the door.

Grace carried the still-wailing Robby into the living room and surveyed the scene. A pretend-kitchen play-set was in the middle of the room, and strewn all around it were pieces of plastic food. A baby walker, the kind that looks like a tiny plastic lawn mower and helps babies stand on two feet, was lying on its side. The couch cushions were balanced between the couch and the coffee table, creating a tunnel beneath.

"Hi, guys!" called Grace over Robby's heaving sobs. "Can you help me look for Robby's pa—um, bink—um, weesie?"

The two kids obligingly hopped down from the couch and began crawling around the floor, looking under all the furniture. At last Ellie gave a triumphant shriek and pointed to the dog. "Rosie has the weesie!"

Sure enough, the dog had found the thing under the coffee table–cushion fort and was carrying it in her mouth. After a thorough rinse, Grace shoved it into Robby's mouth and order was restored.

By the time she heard Mr. Orben's key in the front lock at around nine fifteen, the kids were sound asleep in their beds. Grace had collapsed on the couch watching some dumb reality show on low volume. But the good thing was, Mr. Orben paid her twenty-five dollars.

$37 + $64 for Boomer + $25 = $126.
Add $50 for Palmer dog—$176!
ALMOST THERE!!!

Chapter Five

On Sunday at four, Grace was up in her room, sitting on the floor and peering out at the street. Why weren't they here yet? Already there wasn't that much time to get this project done. She'd cleared off her art table to make room for the big, square piece of plywood that her father had cut for her down in the basement. He'd helped her lug it upstairs even though her mom had suggested they just do the project down in the basement, where it wouldn't be such a big deal if they made a mess. There was no way she would invite the girls down there, though. There was no telling what kind of embarrassing family junk they would see.

She hadn't taken the supplies out of the bag from the

craft store yet because she didn't want to look too eager. She could do that when they got there. But when would that be? It was now 4:07.

At last, at 4:17, a shiny blue SUV pulled into the driveway. Grace jumped onto her bed and opened up a fashion magazine. Better to act like she was in no big rush to start the project. She heard a knock at the front door and her mom letting the girls in. She muttered a silent prayer that her mom wouldn't say anything embarrassing.

When the girls came into her room, Grace slowly closed the magazine and sat up, looking slightly surprised, as though she'd just remembered they were coming. She knew she had to give them a few minutes to walk around her room and check out her stuff before they could start working.

Ashley seemed more curious than Lindsay. Lindsay just gave the room a cursory look and then plunked down in Grace's art chair. Ashley wandered around, picking stuff up from Grace's dresser and putting it down again. "Nice room," she said, although she didn't look all that enthusiastic.

"Oh, thanks," said Grace, trying to sound casual. But suddenly the purple wall color she'd thought was so cool looked stupid and babyish. Her eyes flickered to the stain on the coverlet from when she and her brother had been messing around and he'd spilled some of his sports drink. Should she point it out and explain that it was just sports drink and not anything more embarrassing? No. Keep quiet. Grace's eyes darted over to her bookcase. Why hadn't she cleared out the babyish books? She still had practically a whole shelf of books that she'd read way back in elementary school; books about princesses and kid detectives and even some little-kid jokes and riddles books. Inward groan. She couldn't bring herself to look at the paint stains on the carpet near her art area.

"Ugh. Why can't summer just be here already," complained Lindsay, obviously bored by the tour.

"Stop whining," Ashley said, smiling. "Let's just get this over with."

Grace dragged over two chairs for her and Ashley. Finally she began pulling stuff out of the bag from the craft store.

"I did a little light sketching already, but you guys can change it around if you want. It's just some circles and squares and stuff," said Grace, speaking quickly because she was nervous.

Lindsay didn't even look at the board. She sighed, leaned back, and ran her fingers through her butter-colored hair, twisting it into a ponytail and letting it drop again. "I am so not artistic," she said.

Ashley stood up and looked at Grace's design. "Wow, this is awesome, Grace. You're so talented."

Grace thrilled with pleasure. "It's no big deal. You just make a bunch of circles with a protractor and a bunch of squares with a T square ruler."

Lindsay glanced at her phone and smiled. "Alex says he's going to wear a red shirt!" She giggled. "We're going to match!" Her thumbs zoomed around the keypad as she typed a message back.

Ashley pulled out her own phone and began texting someone, too.

Grace set down the bottle of glue she'd just picked up. "So I went online and did some research on how to do this? Real mandalas aren't glued down, of course. The monks sweep them away to show the impermanence of life. . . ." She trailed off. Both Ashley and Lindsay were staring at her as though she'd suddenly started speaking in Chinese or something. "Anyway," she went on, "what you do is, you put glue down, then sprinkle colored sand and let it dry. Then you do another section. It takes a while because you have to wait for the one color to dry before you do the other. Then when it's all done, what you do is, you spray the whole thing with hairspray and that sets it so the sand won't fall off when you prop it up."

The other two girls barely glanced at the board. "That sounds good," said Lindsay. "Since you're so awesome at the art stuff, why don't you do that and we'll give the presentation, because we're both going to be actresses, so we're good public speakers."

Grace blinked. Then she nodded.

"Hey! I bet since you did all that research, you probably have notes we can use for our report, right?" Ashley asked Grace.

Grace walked heavily over to the binders spilled across the floor on the other side of her bed and took her notes out of her social studies binder. "Here's some research notes I took on Friday," she murmured, handing it over to Ashley.

"Awesome. So we'll do the presenting and you can make the manda-thingummy, okay?"

Grace nodded. Now she was starting to feel anger rising up inside. She was mad at Ashley and Lindsay for making her do most of the work. Mad at herself for not sticking up for herself. And for kidding herself about why they had wanted her to be in their group. It wasn't because they liked her or wanted to be her friend. It was because they knew she'd do a good job on the project. She was such a dork. And yet. A tiny part of her was happy to be in the group no matter what. Maybe now that they'd seen Mike Morris talk to her, they'd change their minds about her dorkiness, at least a little bit.

By the time Mr. Karcher's car horn beeped in the driveway and Grace's mom called upstairs to say it was time for the girls to go, Grace had only finished two colors.

"Cool stuff today, Grace," Ashley said casually. "I'm glad Christina's mom made her invite you to the mall. Yesterday was fun, especially seeing you talk to that Mike Morris guy."

As Lindsay and Ashley bounded out of her room, Grace could feel her stomach sink deep into her carpet. So Mel was right. Christina's mom *had* made Christina include her. Christina certainly didn't care about her. Grace could feel the tears welling up in her eyes. She turned back to the mandala hoping to forget about her embarrassment and concentrate on her schoolwork.

When Grace's dad called her down for dinner, she'd finished a third color, and the mandala was starting to look pretty cool.

"Did you girls get a lot accomplished today?" her mother asked as she put a spoonful of broccoli on Grace's plate.

Grace reached for the bottle of dressing. It was the only way she could force down broccoli, by dipping it into a big puddle of ranch. "Yeah, I have a little more work to do tonight," she said. "I'm doing the visual stuff, and they're going to do the presentation stuff because they know how shy I am and that I hate speaking in public."

"Public speaking is an important skill," grunted her father, helping himself to another piece of chicken.

Why was it that practically everything parents uttered sounded like a lecture?

The phone rang as Grace was clearing the table. The ID said "Alison Clifford." It was Jaci. Grace let it ring a second time so she wouldn't seem too eager.

"Hey," Jaci said. "So tomorrow is supposed to be sunny and seventy-six. Do you want to hang out with me at RSC after school?"

"Definitely, yeah!" Grace was tempted to shout, but she managed to respond more casually. "That sounds good. I'll ask my mom, but I'm sure that's fine."

"Great. Bring your suit and a towel, and goggles if you want to do actual swimming. And you know you don't have to worry about sunblock. I'll bring my usual gallon of it. I wish I didn't burn so easily."

Grace suspected that Jaci was the only middle-school-aged kid on the planet who actually remembered to apply sunblock without being asked, let alone packed it in her bag. But Grace was so psyched to be returning to RSC, she didn't care if she had to use half a bottle of the stuff. "See you tomorrow," she said. She stared into space, an image of Mike floating before her eyes. Maybe they'd run into each other at the snack bar. She wondered if he loved french fries as much as she did. She thought about how his voice sounded as smooth as warmed honey.

Grace's mom and dad were okay with her going, but Grace knew it meant she'd have to finish most of the mandala tonight. But first, Boomer.

As she let herself into the Barbers' house, she got ready for the Boomer onslaught—she braced herself with her knees slightly bent, hands outstretched to ward off his big, slobbery kisses as he dive-bombed into her. But tonight Boomer just padded quietly into the kitchen, his back end wagging only slightly.

"What's up with you, buddy?" she asked, bending down to pet him. Instead of jumping around, he just lowered his head and let her pet him, then raised it and gave her hand a gentle lick.

She looked over at his dish and saw that it was full of food. Startled, she wondered if her mom had said she would feed him tonight and that she simply hadn't paid any attention. But no, that couldn't be. Grace had the only spare key.

"Was something wrong with your breakfast, Boom-Boom?" She dumped out the food, wiped the bowl, and put two new scoops in. But instead of racing to the dish and gulping it down, Boomer just stood there, wanly wagging his tail. "Okay, so let's go for a walk, and then we'll see if you get an appetite."

Back home half an hour later, Grace told her parents about Boomer's lack of appetite. "It's not like him," she said. "He never leaves food in his dish."

"That's odd," said her mom, who was sitting on the floor, sorting through piano books. "Does that sound odd to you, Rusty?"

Her father looked up from the brief he was reading. "Could be any number of things," he said. "See how he's feeling tomorrow morning. If he doesn't seem better, we'll call their vet and ask them what to do."

Grace spent the rest of the evening working on the mandala. It was almost eleven thirty when she finally turned out the light, exhausted. She would have loved to take a hot bath—the next best thing to diving down into a deep pool—but she was too tired. Her last thought before she fell asleep was that her bed was all gritty with sand.

Chapter Six

Grace dreamed she was standing in front of the class, presenting the mandala project all by herself. She realized she'd left her note cards at home. Then when she held it up to show the class, all the sand spilled off onto the floor. She'd forgotten, in her dream, to glue down the sand. Then she looked down and saw that she had no shoes or socks on. And she was in her underwear!

Her alarm blasted her awake with its totally horrible *beh-beh-beh!*—she'd set it from radio to alarm the night before, knowing it would be hard to wake up. Bleary and fogged, with that awful empty feeling of not having had enough sleep, she crawled out of bed, picked some shorts and a sweatshirt off the floor, and pulled them on.

When she got to the Barbers' house, she peered through the window into the kitchen and saw Boomer splayed across the kitchen floor, asleep. He roused himself when she opened the door, but his food dish was still half-full.

"Feeling a little better?" she said, clipping the leash to his collar. He wagged his back end cheerfully. But when they went for a walk, he didn't pull on the leash at all. Walking Boomer was usually like water skiing—he'd pull her in his wake and she'd hang on for dear life. Today he walked demurely at her side and seemed to be limping on one of his front legs. She squatted down and asked for his paw, and he sat down and lifted it up for her so she could examine the pad. But there didn't seem to be anything in the way of a cut or a thorn. She petted his face with a hand on each side of his muzzle, not even really minding the drool too much.

"Hey. Are your ears warm, Boomer?" she asked him.

He cocked his head to one side, as though trying to decide if they were or if they were not.

"I think your ears feel warm," she said. "Maybe that means you have a little doggie temperature. Don't worry. I'm going to tell my mom and she'll call the doctor."

Grace reported Boomer's symptoms to her mother at breakfast.

"Hmm," said her mother. "That certainly doesn't sound

like Boomer. Leave me the key to get in, and I'll call the Barbers' vet as soon as the office is open."

As Grace hurried to her room to pack up her backpack, she thought ruefully about how late she'd stayed up working on the mandala. Well, it was mostly finished, so that was good, as it was due the day after tomorrow. She grabbed her old one-piece suit from her top drawer, then stopped and put it back. What if she saw Mike Morris at RSC today? It would not be good if she had on her faded, stretched-out blue one-piece. Plus she looked like a little kid in it. Rummaging around in the drawer, she fished out the new two-piece she and her mom had bought at last year's end-of-season sales. Would it fit her? It had been laughably big in the chest last August, but now, well, at least she'd made *some* progress in that department since then. Humming to herself, she picked up her new barrettes and clipped her hair back from her face. *Not too bad*, she thought, looking at her reflection in the mirror. She stuffed the suit into her pack, along with a towel. She was going to RSC! She might see Mike! With a little skip, she trotted off to catch the bus.

Grace was trying to shove her bulging backpack into her locker as Christina approached her own locker. "Cute barrettes. Very retro. Tough hair day today?" Christina asked.

Grace made a silent vow never to wear these stupid barrettes ever again. They did make her look like a little kid. Why did Christina always have to point stuff like that out, though?

"How did it go yesterday?" Christina asked as she spun the combination lock.

Grace gritted her teeth and smiled. She wasn't going to let Christina know that she knew that her mom had forced Christina to invite Grace to the mall. "Fine. We didn't get as much done as we wanted because we ran out of time. The glue took a long time to dry between colors."

Christina furrowed her brow. "Glue? What are you talking about?"

"Our mandala project. The one with Ashley and Lindsay."

"Oooooh." She giggled. "No, I meant your planning for the dance. Have you got everything all set with your dress and your shoes and stuff?"

A sketch Grace had doodled of Mike Morris in math on Friday fell out of her locker. She grabbed it and shoved it inside her notebook. Had Christina seen it? "Oh. Right. The dance. I'm wearing my cousin Candace's dress."

"Candace? I've met her before at your house, right?

The one who's a freshman at college with a hot younger brother? Hasn't Candace got, like, a totally amazing body?" Christina's gaze flickered up and down Grace's body. "How on earth are *you* going to wear *her* dress?"

Grace flushed. "It fits me fine," she said, even though it didn't. When Christina didn't say anything, she added, "And I'm going to wear my black wedge sandals."

Christina pressed her lips together. "Surely you don't intend to wear those platform ones that make you taller than ninety-seven percent of the boys in our grade."

Did Christina take a mean pill this morning? Grace wondered. Was she trying to say as many nasty things as possible in the three minutes before the bell rang? Thank goodness she had Mel to go to the dance with.

"So guess who asked me to the dance?" Christina gushed, taking hold of Grace's arm, suddenly back to her warm, friendly self.

"Why don't you tell me?" Grace already knew the answer because she'd overheard Ashley at the mall and she still felt a little stung that Christina wasn't sharing the news with her until now . . . and that she didn't have a date.

"Only *Max,* that's who! OMG!" She gave a tiny squeal and hopped up and down, still holding on to Grace's arm. "He's *totally* the hottest guy at Lincoln Middle School!" Then she gave Grace a serious look. "Have you had any luck?"

"Luck? With what?"

"You know. Has anyone asked you to the dance? Wait. Don't answer. That wasn't nice. Of course not."

Now Grace's whole body stiffened. She'd had it with Christina. "What's that supposed to mean? Like it's totally and completely out of the question that someone would ask me to the dance?"

Christina frowned. "I didn't mean it like that. You're so sensitive these days. No offense, but maybe if you wore a little makeup, you might, you know, be a little more popular with the guys."

Grace wheeled around to face Christina, her fists jammed into her sides. "You can be really mean sometimes."

Christina's eyes widened. Her mouth dropped open. "We've been friends for, like, ever. I thought we could say anything to each other. Who's going to be honest and tell you that you dress like a dork if not your true friends?"

"Well, maybe that's not the kind of 'true friend' I need," said Grace. Her words hung in the air between them. Then the bell rang. Grace slammed her locker closed and hurried off to homeroom. As upset as she was with Christina, Grace couldn't help but feel a little swell of pride for finally standing up for herself.

Chapter Seven

Despite the fact that it was a Monday, with nine days still left in the school year, the entire school seemed to have caught summer fever. Even the teachers acted restless and distracted. Classroom windows were thrown open, and the warm, sunny breeze wafted gently inside, bringing with it smells of lilacs, freshly mowed grass, and the promise of summer. By the time the final bell rang and the hallways filled with chattering students and bleary-eyed teachers, Grace felt like she couldn't get outside fast enough. She and Jaci met at the bike rack and waited for Jaci's mother to show up.

"There she is," Jaci said as a shiny silver car pulled up to the curb.

Grace didn't know much about cars, but she could tell this was a fancy one. Come to think of it, she didn't know much about Jaci, either, outside of Spanish class. Jaci opened the back door and shoved Grace in ahead of her, then got in herself. The car smelled of expensive leather and a heavenly perfume, like flowers and spices combined.

"Mom, this is my friend Grace," Jaci said flatly.

Jaci's mom turned around and smiled at Grace. If Grace were casting a movie and held an audition for the part of Jaci's mom, this woman wouldn't even have gotten a callback. She looked like the exact opposite of her daughter. Jaci herself was completely no-frills. Her light-brown hair was always pulled back in a careless ponytail, and her wire-rimmed glasses were completely boring and functional—not like Mel's, which were all about making a fashion statement. And Jaci's clothes were totally whatever—they made Grace look like a fashionista. Jaci's mom, on the other hand, was the most glamorous mom Grace had ever seen. She wore a huge pair of sunglasses, and her glossy hair was cut in an expensive and ultracool style. Her perfect nose, full lips, and flawless skin made her look like a movie star.

"Hello, Grace," she said. Her smile revealed impossibly

white, perfect teeth. "So nice for Jaci to have a friend to go to the club with today!"

Jaci groaned and rolled her eyes. "Mom, please," she said. "Grace has been there with me twice already."

Grace gaped at Jaci. How on earth could Jaci possibly act like she was annoyed by such a perfect mother? Not only was Mrs. Clifford gorgeous; she was also nice! Grace was almost positive that Jaci's mom didn't make her earn her membership to RSC.

"Have a great time, girls," said Mrs. Clifford as she dropped them off. "Remember, Mrs. Cabrera is officially in charge of you. She'll be over at the kiddie-pool area, but I called the front desk and told them. I'll be back for you around five."

As Jaci's mom drove away, Jaci shook her head. "Sorry about my mom. So annoying sometimes."

"I thought she was pretty nice," Grace ventured.

"She's okay, I guess. But she is putting serious pressure on me to go to the dance." Jaci flashed her ID at the young woman at the front desk and then slid a piece of paper across the desk. Grace knew it was a guest pass. The woman nodded and waved them through, and the two girls headed toward the locker room to change. "My week is busy enough as it is, without having to go to some dumb dance. I have my big clarinet recital on Saturday, and I have a lot of practicing to do."

Grace suppressed a grin. Jaci was probably the only middle schooler she knew who practiced without being nagged by a parent. It was amazing that Jaci could think her mother was embarrassing. Grace thought she was the coolest mom she'd ever met. Maybe you lost all perspective when it came to your own parents, no matter how cool they actually were. She tried to imagine if anyone on earth would consider her own parents cool. It seemed highly unlikely.

Before they went into the locker room, Grace looked quickly around, hoping for a glimpse of Mike. But he was nowhere to be seen.

The RSC locker room was quite a contrast to the one at school—this one was clean and shiny and there was nothing written inside the lockers and no junk thrown onto the floor. Luckily there were individual changing rooms, so Grace could try on her new two-piece without Jaci watching. They entered side-by-side rooms and continued talking.

"So you're not going?" Grace said as she pulled on her bikini bottom. It fit, thank goodness.

"I so don't want to go," Jaci replied. "What's fun about

standing around in uncomfortable clothes, eating bad food, and watching our classmates try to dance?"

Grace hooked her bathing suit top closed, then swiveled the clasp around to the back and lifted it up to tie it around her neck. She flinched at her reflection in the mirror. The top was still pretty big. It would totally gap if she leaned over even a little. She tried to spread the gathered part at the bottom as wide as it would go, then tied it as tightly as she could at the back of her neck. She looked completely stupid, and her neck hurt where the knot was tied. She grabbed her towel and fastened it around herself at the chest level. Now she looked like she was wearing a terry-cloth muumuu. The only thing to do was pray she didn't see anyone she knew.

They emerged from the dressing rooms at almost exactly the same time. Jaci had on a black one-piece suit, her towel draped casually over one arm. She didn't say anything to Grace about the towel muumuu as they walked out to the pool deck. Jaci seemed the opposite of Christina in that respect—she just couldn't care less about what she or anyone else was wearing.

They found two chairs in the sun, and Grace unwrapped her towel, draped it on the chair, and clambered onto it, lying back quickly in such a way that her bathing suit top wouldn't gap. She'd just settled into the chair when her cell rang.

"Hi, honey," said her mom. "You were right about Boomer! They did a blood test on him and the poor thing has Lyme disease. They said it was great of you to be so heads-up, and they were able to catch it early enough that he should be just fine. They gave me some pills, which you have to give him once a day."

"Oh, that's good," said Grace, trying not to sound too proud, although secretly she was. "I'll talk to you later, okay?"

Her mother must have gotten the message that Grace couldn't talk in public, because she signed off quickly.

"What was that about?" asked Jaci, slathering gobs of sunblock onto her freckly white legs. She offered the bottle to Grace, who hesitated for a second but took it.

"Oh, just a dog I'm taking care of for a job."

"That's so cool that you have a job," said Jaci. "I've applied for a job too, so I won't have to spend all summer lying around this place all day every day. Have you decided to join?"

For some reason Grace didn't want to go into detail about earning her own membership money. "I'm ninety percent sure I'll probably join," she said casually, mentally tallying for the nineteenth time that day how much more she had to earn toward her membership.

"I hope you do," said Jaci, lying back in her chair and pulling a thick book out of her bag. She opened an oversize glasses case and swapped her wire-rimmed glasses for her large pair of prescription sunglasses.

"Yes, I—" Grace stopped midsentence. Mike Morris was coming their way! She resisted a wild impulse to throw her tote bag over herself to cover up her too-large bathing suit top, but she couldn't have done that even if she wanted to, as she was frozen to the chair with nervousness. Her knuckles got white as she watched him turn the corner at the edge of the pool and head straight for them.

Grace shimmied up the chair a millimeter at a time until she was more or less sitting up. Her bathing suit hadn't slipped down or sideways.

"Tsup," said Mike, stopping in front of their chairs.

"Hello," said Jaci, and there was something about the fact that she said "hello" rather than "hi" that made Grace feel uncomfortable. It was a little formal and unfriendly.

There was an awkward moment. Then Mike spoke. "Grace, right?"

She nodded. Then she recovered enough to say, "This is Jaci."

Mike leaned down and offered his hand. Jaci looked a little taken aback, but she shook his hand. "Sorry if I slimed you," she said. "I just applied sunblock."

"Can't be too careful, can you?" said Mike easily. "Last thing you want is a bad sunburn this early in the year."

Jaci nodded her head slowly, as though trying to decide if he was making fun of her or not. "Rrrrrriiiight," she said.

Mike turned to Grace. "So, you been doing much diving recently?" he asked.

"Oh! Yes! I mean, no, not today. I can't today. I, um, can't go in the water today." Inward cringe. He probably thought it was that time of the month, even though she hadn't even gotten her period yet. Or that she had some horrible skin condition that prevented her from going into the water. Why didn't she just come right out and tell him she couldn't go in because her bathing suit would fall off if she dove in, because she'd had to buy it on sale and, oh, by the way, she also didn't have enough to fill it out on top?

"Okay, cool. Well, see you around," he said, and loped away toward the snack bar.

Grace closed her eyes, breathless with mortification.

"Please tell me I didn't sound like a total, utter idiot," she said to Jaci.

Jaci looked at her with surprise. "Why on earth would I think that?"

Grace sighed. "No reason."

Chapter Eight

By Tuesday morning Boomer already seemed better. He barreled into her as she stepped into the kitchen and tried to dance around her several times as she attempted to wade over to his food dish without falling over. She put a little peanut butter on his pill and let him sniff it. He agreeably devoured it whole, licking the peanut butter from his lips a little uncertainly. When she put the scoop of food into his dish, he immediately gobbled it down in his usual Boomer-like way.

"Looks like you're feeling better, huh, Boom?" she said, and tousled the fur behind his ears. He was still the dumbest, slobberiest canine in the western hemisphere, but she was growing pretty attached to him, she had to admit.

At lunchtime Mel announced to Grace that she couldn't go to the dance.

Grace stopped sketching a picture of Mike on her napkin. She turned toward Mel, horror written across her face. "Why? Why not?"

Mel sighed. "My mom is insisting we go visit my cousins for the weekend," she said. "Since we're going to be away so much this summer, it's the only time we can go. I'm sorry, Grace. Can you go with Christina?"

Grace's gaze swiveled over to where Christina was sitting at the center table, surrounded by popular girls. "I think she's got a date," she said miserably. "*All* those girls have dates. This is a disaster, an absolute catastrophe."

Mel clearly knew she was right. All she could do was say she was sorry.

Grace didn't feel much like finishing her lunch. She mumbled something to Mel about needing to get to her locker early, and cleared her stuff.

"Sorry again," Mel called after her. "I'll see you tonight for my birthday dinner, though, okay? We'll pick you up at six."

Grace nodded miserably and made her way out of the

cafeteria. She walked through the hallway, lost in thought, her head down, and nearly collided head-on with someone who smelled strongly of a manly brand of body spray. It was only by windmilling her arms wildly and teetering as though at the edge of a cliff that she managed to regain her balance and not bump into him. And of course, it would have to be Max Mosello, the hottest guy in the school . . . and Christina's date to the dance.

"Hey, Grace."

He knew her name? She resisted the temptation to look behind her, to see if he might be addressing another person named Grace standing in the background. But no, he was looking straight at her, Grace Davis.

"Hi," she managed.

"I was just coming to see you at the cafeteria—we have the same lunch period. So Christina tells me you're quite the artist."

Now she really must be dreaming. Why would he have noticed that they were in lunch together? And why would Christina have said something nice about her to the hottest guy in the school, especially after the fight they'd had yesterday? Since then they'd barely spoken to each other. "Yeah, I like to draw and stuff. Just for fun. I—"

"Sure. That's great," Max broke in. "Well, I have a

business proposition for you. I'm kind of in a jam with my geography project in Mr. Lewis's class, and it's due tomorrow. We're studying Canada, and I'm supposed to write about the province of Saskatchewan. I know, right? Who cares about Saskatchewan?"

With her lips covering her teeth to hide her braces, Grace smiled and nodded quickly, so he would be sure to know that *she* certainly didn't care about Saskatchewan.

"I was thinking maybe you could help me write it and then do some kind of presentation board."

Grace jumped. For tomorrow? No way. She was pretty well finished with the mandala, and Ashley and Lindsay had assured her that the presentation was all set, but still. She'd have to do a bunch of research for this. It could take all night.

"Don't worry. I'm not assuming you'd do this for nothing!" He smiled at her in such a warm, heart-meltingly friendly way, his handsome face revealing impossibly adorable dimples, his big eyes so brown and limpid that she thought she could fall into them like a vat of melted chocolate. Not quite at the Mike Morris level, but pretty close, she had to concede. "I'll pay you fifty bucks, cash, up front. Look, see? I have it right here." He opened his wallet and peeled out a fifty-dollar bill. Grace couldn't help but notice that he had quite a few more bills in the fold of his wallet.

She snapped out of her reverie about his beautiful brown eyes. Fifty dollars! Her mind began rapidly calculating. She already had $126. With the prospect of twenty-five dollars from the Orbens on Saturday, the fifty from the Palmer dog sitting job, plus this fifty dollars, she'd be way over two hundred by the end of the coming weekend! "What do you need me to do?" she asked eagerly.

"Um, well, I haven't actually started it yet. But that makes it easier for you, right? Blank slate and all. What's cool about it is, you can choose anything you want to do. I told Mr. Lewis it was going to be a big surprise."

"Well, I have a bunch of different-colored felt squares," said Grace thoughtfully. "It could be fun to make a big flag from the province. Something like that." As she thought about it she became more excited about the possibilities. "Then I could research what the natural resources are and maybe make a little cutout for each corner, surrounding the flag." The more she thought about what she could do, the more eager she became.

Still, a nagging thought kept tugging away at her. She tried to ignore it, but it kept tugging. It was telling her this was wrong. This was illegal. This was cheating. They could both get in huge trouble if anyone found out. She pushed that tugging thought as far back into the corner of her mind as she could. First of all, no one would find out. Second— this was Max Mosello, asking *her* for a big favor! He was the core of the core group of popular kids. If she did this, she'd be in. Maybe they'd even invite her to sit with them at lunch! And go to the dance in a big, popular-kid group!

"Sure, okay," she said with a shy smile. "Why don't you give me your notes and stuff and I'll see what I can do."

Max's face lit up with delight and he pumped the air with his fist. "Yesssss! Grace, you are the greatest. Now I can go to the concert tonight."

Grace gave him another wan smile, but inside she got all clenched up. There it was again—this concert everyone in the world was going to except for her. And Mel, of course, but Mel didn't seem to mind being a borderline social outcast.

Max took out his phone, glanced from side to side to be sure no teachers were in sight, and sent someone a quick text. Then he put it back in his pocket and reached out for her hand. Confused, she held out her hand and he clasped it, pressing the folded fifty-dollar bill into her palm. She pulled her hand back and stared at the money in disbelief. She had the money! Her summer was really looking up!

"Meet me at my locker as soon as the last bell rings," he

said with the air of someone used to getting others to do what he commanded. "I'll give you the assignment sheet and my notebook and stuff." The hallway was now crowded with kids hurrying to class. "You're the best, Grace," he said with another huge smile, and walked away, leaving Grace drenched in the smell of body spray.

She didn't have time to get to her locker before social studies. But arriving without the textbook was probably okay because they were going to be doing group work for the projects, which were due tomorrow. As she stepped into the classroom, her eyes fell on Mel and a thought struck her like a bolt of lightning. *Mel. Tonight. Birthday dinner with her grandmother. Oh no.*

Grace dropped her backpack on her desk and then hurried over to Mel, who was unrolling a large piece of poster board with Rashid and Chris. They'd shoved four desks together to make a large work surface. Grace plucked Mel's shirt to tell her they had to talk, and Mel stepped aside.

"What's up?" asked Mel. "Are you still upset about the dance? Listen I'm so sorry, but my mom—"

"No, it's fine," Grace interrupted. She lowered her voice.

"It's just that . . . something came up since I saw you, and I can't go to dinner with you tonight." Grace looked away. She couldn't meet Mel's eyes.

"Something came up? Since I saw you in the cafeteria? That was like sixteen minutes ago."

"Yeah, I know. I, um." Grace spoke in a low voice so Ms. Holmes wouldn't hear her. "I promised to help someone with his school assignment, and it's due tomorrow so I'm, um, we're going to be working really late."

"Whose school assignment?" Mel asked bluntly. Grace wished she wouldn't talk so that anyone could hear.

"Max Mosello's," Grace said, almost whispering.

Mel's eyes widened. "You're working on a project with Max Mosello? I didn't know you guys even had any classes together."

"We don't, except lunch."

"So how are you working on a project with him?"

"It's not exactly with him. It's . . . for him."

Mel narrowed her eyes. "What are you up to?"

"Nothing. I told him I'd help him out with the art part of a project he has to do, and, well, it's due tomorrow."

Mel crossed her arms, then drummed her fingers along her lower lip. "Is he making you do it for him?"

"No!" Grace said quickly.

"There's a big concert tonight," Mel said thoughtfully. "A whole bunch of kids are going. Is he going?"

"How should I know?" said Grace hotly. She hated lying to her friend. But why should she get so worried about what Mel might think, after Mel had abandoned her to go to the dance alone?

Mel shrugged. "Okay. Whatever. Grammy was psyched to see you. Christina already blew me off because of the stupid concert. Obviously her priorities are really messed up these days, but I thought yours weren't. Guess I was wrong."

She spun on her heel and headed back to her work space with Rashid and Chris.

Grace's stomach felt like she'd swallowed a stone. Why couldn't she be as strong and sure of herself as Mel? Why did she care so much what other people thought of her? She trudged over to where Lindsay and Ashley were sitting with their heads together, whispering and giggling.

Ashley pushed a piece of paper across the desk to show to Grace. "Here's what we did in study hall yesterday. What do you think?"

Grace tried to swallow the huge lump in her throat, but it was stuck. She stared down at the half page of loopy handwriting. There were about three sentences of basic information about what a mandala is. Grace cleared her throat, praying her voice wouldn't betray her abject misery. "Um, it's a pretty good start? But, um, maybe we should add a little something more about its significance to Buddhists?"

"Great idea," said Lindsay. "Add whatever you want, and type it up in a large font. Ash and I will do the talking tomorrow. That's what you wanted, right? You hate speaking in public, don't you? Well, not to worry. We make a great team!" She bared her teeth in what passed for a smile.

Grace pulled out her notebook, flipped it open, and began writing the presentation.

Chapter Nine

By the time social studies was over, the little tugging thought at the back of Grace's mind had grown into a major tug-of-war inside her head. Grace realized there was no way she could go through with the plan Max had outlined. She'd have to tell him no and give him back the money.

She fretted all through science. By the time Spanish rolled around, she could barely register Señora Pereira's instructions for homework. When the final bell rang, she had started to tremble. As she walked through the hallways to meet Max at his locker, her mouth felt dry and she resisted the urge to gag. What if she threw up right on the floor in front of him? Maybe a tornado would touch down and they'd have to evacuate the school, and all of tomorrow's classes would be canceled. Or maybe she could figure out a way to faint on the spot and have to be rushed to the hospital in an ambulance. But fate refused to cooperate and she found herself approaching Max at his locker chatting with a group of kids. When he saw Grace he waved the kids aside like a Roman emperor, and they obediently melted away.

"Hey, Grace. Got my notes for you. Got the assignment sheet. Got—"

"I can't do it," she blurted out. "I can't help you with your assignment." She held out the crumpled bill and looked away so she wouldn't have to see his face. "Something came up and now I—well, I just can't."

She darted a look at him. He was staring at her in disbelief, the anger creeping up from his collar line and spreading across his face so dramatically she could actually see it happening, like one of those time-lapse photography videos of clouds moving across the sun and the world growing rapidly darker.

When he didn't take the money, she thrust it onto the upper shelf of his locker, then dropped her hand at her side.

"But I'm supposed to go to a concert in a few minutes," he spluttered.

"I know. I'm sorry. I'm really so sorry."

Max's brown eyes now practically sent out sparks of

fury. How different they looked from what she'd seen after lunch. "Well, great. That's just great. Thanks for nothing," he said through barely clenched teeth.

She raced away, praying she wouldn't burst into tears in the middle of the hallway.

A few minutes later she was on the bus, slumped into an empty seat and stared out the window, hoping no one would see her. Her phone vibrated and she pulled it out of her pocket. Through blurred vision she saw that it was a text from her mom saying the Palmers had called and said they didn't need her to take care of their dog after all. Suddenly *that* fifty dollars she'd counted on was no longer available. Now she'd never get the money for the membership.

Luckily her mom wasn't in the kitchen when Grace opened the door and stepped inside. She didn't want to face her mother, who could always tell when Grace was upset. The first thing Grace did was find the Orbens' number on the side of the fridge. No one was home, so she left a message on their machine, trying to keep her voice from quavering, saying that she would be able to babysit on Friday after all. That was that. She was definitely not going to the dance.

As Grace walked through the dining room and up the

stairs, she could hear her mom giving a piano lesson in the living room. From the sound of the piece, halting and simple, the student was a little kid. That made sense since they got out of school earlier than middle schoolers.

She threw herself onto her bed and thought about how nice it would be to still be in elementary school. She had a flashback to second grade, when she and Christina and Mel had been in the same classroom, taken the same gymnastics class, even had the same pediatrician. Everything was so much simpler then. Now Mel was mad at her, and she and Christina weren't even speaking. Seven more days of school left in the year. Could she survive? Maybe her dad could get transferred to another city.

Her phone buzzed, and she checked the caller. It was Christina. She almost didn't pick up, but at the last second clicked the button. "Hi," she said, sounding guarded.

"Grace. What were you thinking?" Christina was obviously really mad.

"I know," said Grace in a tiny voice.

"I totally set up the whole thing for you. I felt bad about our fight and wanted to do something *nice* for you! I told him you were this awesome artist, and I thought you'd be psyched to be included and stuff. And then you *bailed* on him? Think how you made *me* look!"

Grace started picking at her fingernail polish. She sat up, then lay back down. It was all she could do not to cry.

"Are you there?"

"Yes."

"I don't understand why you've changed so much. You don't seem to want to participate in anything fun anymore. No offense, but a lot of people think you're stuck-up."

Kids thought *she* was stuck-up? That was crazy. What would she have to be stuck-up *about*? "That's so not true" was all Grace could manage.

Christina sighed. "Max is mad at *me* now. What if he uninvites me to the dance?"

"I've decided not to go," said Grace.

"Humph." Christina didn't seem a bit surprised. "That's probably a good idea. Anyway, I have to go. Bye." She hung up without even waiting for Grace to say good-bye.

She stared at the phone in her hand. Then she texted Mel.

RU mad? I'm free tonite if u still want me to come with u. O and i'm not going 2 the dance.

With a heavy sigh, she rolled onto her side and tried to doze.

About ten minutes later her phone buzzed. It was a text from Mel.

I asked Emily and she's coming instead. Sry.

So that was that. She now officially had no friends left on the planet.

Chapter Ten

Grace woke up with an awful headache and stomachache. Did she have the flu? Then she remembered what
had happened the day before. Right. So she didn't have
a deadly disease, but maybe that would have been better than what was actually the matter—no one at Lincoln
Middle School was speaking to her. She was about as welcome as a skunk at a barbecue.

She put on slightly nicer clothes than she usually wore
to school: blue jeans that weren't frayed at the bottom, a
purple blouse that hugged her waist and tied at the back,
her wedge sandals. She even put stuff in her hair to smooth
it down.

But of course Boomer chose today to outdo himself in
the slobber department. He managed to wrap big strings

of drool around her pant leg and, when they came inside from their walk, to put a huge, muddy paw on the back of her blouse as she was bending over to put food into his dish. So when she got back to her house, she had to race upstairs to change, and everything was either wrinkled or dirty or missing something important, like buttons. Finally she threw on a skirt that she'd sort of gotten too big for and a wrinkly T-shirt that she wasn't positive was clean.

And then she missed the bus.

But that turned out to be a fortunate thing because as she trudged home from the bus stop, limping a bit from a blister on her little toe from her impractical wedge sandals, she realized she'd completely forgotten she had to bring in the mandala today.

Her mother was on her way out to the dentist when Grace returned from the bus stop, and was deeply displeased that she had to drive Grace to school. It meant calling and rescheduling the dentist appointment—to August.

Then the mandala barely fit into Grace's mom's car and Grace had to hold it on her lap with the seat reclined, so that by the time they got to school her neck was so stiff it felt like she'd been in one of those stockades she had seen while on a third-grade field trip to a pilgrim village.

In homeroom Emily told her all about the fantastic restaurant she and Mel had gone to the previous evening. "We had *the* most amazing dessert," she gushed. "It was, like, a huge piece of chocolate cake filled with molten chocolate that just oozed out onto the plate, and they topped it with gobs of whipped cream. I mean, *gobs*."

Grace smiled weakly, and a rubber band popped off her braces and landed on top of Justin Guerrera's head. Luckily he didn't seem to notice.

She spent the lunch period hiding in the bathroom, and for once didn't even feel hungry. As she walked into the social studies classroom, lugging the mandala, Grace's mind kept flashing back to her nightmare where everything had slid off the board when she held up the mandala. Ashley and Lindsay were already at their desks. Both shot her a chilly look.

"Why don't we start with . . ." Ms. Holmes glanced down at her notes. "Grace, Ashley, and Lindsay."

It figured they'd have to go first. Although the room was air-conditioned, it was such a hot day that Grace had to pry her sweaty legs off the chair as she stood up. Grace followed Ashley and Lindsay to the front of the room. They smiled at Grace and helped her prop the mandala up on the easel, acting for all the world as though the three of them were best friends. Grace had draped a cloth over her design so she could lift it up when it was time to reveal the mandala to the class.

Ashley started out, barely glancing at the paper Grace had typed up. Then Lindsay chimed in. Back and forth they went, acting like they made presentations every day. Of course, they used Grace's research, Grace's notes, Grace's wording. Grace just stared at the floor, feeling embarrassed and idiotic. Still, Grace was forced to admit, they were way better at speaking in front of a group than she would ever be.

"And here," said Lindsay, gesturing toward Grace, "is our mandala, for your viewing pleasure. Of course we had to glue it down, but the real monks would sweep it up and throw it away as a reminder of the impermanence of life."

Grace pulled up the cloth to reveal the mandala. The class oohed and ahhed in a most satisfying way. They got a big round of applause.

When Mel's group presented their Japanese food project, they did a sushi-rolling demonstration for the class, and then everyone got to try some. Grace was amazed at how good it tasted. Plus her appetite had come rushing back. She had four pieces. Mel barely looked at her as she passed the tray around the circle of eager students.

In Spanish they watched a video with a bunch of songs about Spanish grammar. As soon as the lights dimmed, Jaci tapped Grace's shoulder from behind, leaned forward, and whispered, "What's up? You look pretty droopy today."

"I just said yes to babysitting Friday night, so I'm not going to the dance," Grace whispered back dully. "And now I guess I just feel kind of bummed about not going."

"Why would you be bummed about not going?" asked Jaci, looking genuinely baffled. "It's my worst nightmare, listening to bad music played too loud and having sweaty guys tripping over my feet."

"*¡Presten atención, por favor!*" said Señora Pereira.

At least she'd been able to get her dad's money back for the dance ticket. Maybe he'd let her keep it out of pity. Then again, knowing her dad, that wasn't going to happen.

After school Grace practically ran smack into Max and Christina as she rounded the corner of the building on her way to the bus. They were leaning against the side of the building, talking with their heads close together. Max saw her first, and he scowled as he watched her pass them. Christina turned around to see who he was looking at and met Grace's gaze with a neutral expression, then turned back to Max, said something, and giggled.

Grace almost missed the bus home. It was about to pull away and she rapped on the door, making a pleading motion with her hands, and the bus driver glowered at her and opened the door.

About the only bright spot in an otherwise awful day was that at least Boomer was happy to see her. And he seemed completely recovered. She took him for an extra-long walk that night and gave him three treats after he had his pill.

Before bed she calculated her earnings.

$37 savings
$64 for Boomer
$25 for babysitting
= $126
Friday babysitting: $25?
Saturday babysitting: $25?
Total will be $176

Even after all that babysitting she wouldn't meet the goal. Just to torture herself more, she conjured up an image of Mike, tanned and muscled. By the time she finally raised enough money to join, he'd have forgotten she even existed.

It just wasn't fair.

Chapter Eleven

During school on Thursday Grace moved from class to class in a fog. She felt more adrift than she had the first week of middle school, when she'd felt perpetually lost, nervous, and unsure where to look. Now she knew where she was going, of course, but she could almost feel the hostility emanating from people as she passed them in the hallways, like heat shimmering off a barbecue grill on a summer day. Everyone seemed to be talking about the dance. Everyone was going except her, it seemed. At their lockers that morning, Christina had said a curt hello to her. Then she quickly pulled out a book, checked her makeup in her mirror, closed her locker, and left, with a terse "See ya."

Grace spent her lunch period at the nurse's office, claiming she had a stomachache. By the time she got home from school, she was ravenous.

Friday began the same way. She dawdled on purpose after getting off the bus, so she wouldn't have to see Christina at their lockers, and made it to homeroom just before the second bell rang. *At least there's only a few more days in the school year,* she thought gloomily as she took her seat.

The one bright spot in the day came during lunchtime. Grace almost decided to skip it again and hide in the girls' bathroom, but as she'd been able to choke down only a half piece of toast at breakfast, she was too hungry to go without lunch again. As soon as she entered the cafeteria, she spotted Mel, already in the line, who smiled at her. Maybe Mel didn't hate her!

Good old Mel. When Grace emerged from the line, carrying her tray with her heart pounding, she saw Mel waving her over to sit with her.

"I have something for you," Mel said as soon as Grace had sat down. Grace watched Mel pull a small envelope from the back pocket of her jeans.

"What is this?"

"My ticket to the dance tonight. Obviously I'm not using it, so I thought maybe you might have changed your mind about not going. And also my raffle ticket. I thought you could keep it for me, and if I win the scooter, we can share it."

"Oh. Thanks for the offer, but I told the Orbens I would babysit, so there's no way I can go." Grace slid it back toward Mel. "Better give it to someone else."

Mel slid it back toward Grace. "No, you take it. Who else on this planet would I want to share a scooter with? Maybe you'll change your mind. You never know."

Grace was so happy that Mel was speaking to her that she took the envelope and stuffed it into her pocket.

Christina didn't appear at her locker after lunch. Grace felt her phone vibrate. Was it Christina? She slipped it out of her pocket and surreptitiously checked it inside her locker. The text was from her mother.

No babysitting tonight. Robby O. is sick. XO Mom

She shut off her phone. Her first thought was, *There goes another twenty-five dollars I'd counted on for my member-ship*. But then a second thought struck her. She pulled the crumpled envelope out of her pocket and peeked inside at the dance ticket. *No way,* she thought, and shoved it back into her pocket.

Science let out five minutes before the bell rang because Mr. Dawkins had to have a conference call with a parent. So Grace got to Spanish early and stood outside, studying for the last quiz of the school year.

"Grace!" It was Jaci. She breathlessly dropped her heavy backpack at her feet and leaned against the wall next to Grace. "You have *got* to bail me out," she said, wasting no time.

"What's up?"

"It's my mom. She is *insisting* that I go tonight. She says it's important that I spend more time with kids my own age, and if I want to take the job I was just offered, I need to show that I'm willing to 'mingle'"—air quotes—"with my peer group."

"You got a summer job?" Grace couldn't imagine a girl like Jaci spending time walking dogs or mowing lawns. Or why anyone would want to spend the summer doing anything but hanging out at RSC.

Jaci nodded. "It's a volunteer job at the university, in the pigeon lab. I want to work for a professor, helping out with the birds. Just two mornings a week. So anyway, please tell me you don't have a date tonight."

"I wasn't going to go. Remember I said I was baby-sitting? Only, well, one of the kids is sick, so now I'm not."

"Perfect! Then you can go with me!"

"No, see, I wasn't going to *go*. Maybe we can just, like, hang out or something."

"Have you *met* my mom?"

"Yes. She's really nice."

"Well, hidden beneath that 'nice' exterior there lurks a tough-as-nails dictator. Think Napoleon, with a henna hair rinse."

"I don't have anything decent to wear. All I have is a dumb dress from my cousin that doesn't fit."

The bell rang and the door burst open as kids from the previous class streamed out of the room. "I'm sure it's fine," said Jaci. "And if it isn't, you can borrow something from me."

Grace glanced dubiously at Jaci, dressed in unfashionable jeans that were half an inch too short, uncool sneakers with pink-striped socks, and a gray pocket-tee that looked like she'd borrowed it from an older brother. "All right," Grace said as she followed Jaci into the classroom. "I'll ask my mom if she can bring me to your house after school, but no promises. If the dress makes me look like a total dork, then we can just rent a movie and hang out, okay?"

"Sure," said Jaci, although Grace could see that Jaci had very likely inherited the stubborn streak from her mother. Decent dress or no decent dress, Grace had a feeling she'd be going to the dance that night. *Well, it's not like I could drop any lower on the popularity charts,* she thought grimly.

Grace secretly hoped her mom would say no to the idea of her going to the dance with Jaci, but of course, her mom seemed delighted. "I'm glad you have a new friend. You and Jaci seem to be hanging out a lot these days," she said as she chopped a carrot. "Will you be meeting Christina there, then?"

"Sort of," muttered Grace. She hadn't told her mom about her problems with Christina. It was just too complicated.

"Run up and change, and I'll drive you over there before my next student shows up."

The dress made her look like a total dork. Grace stared at herself in the mirror. The brown color of the dress, which had looked so elegant on Candace in the pictures she'd seen at her cousin's house, looked drab and ugly on her. It clashed with her hair, for heaven's sake. It was too short and made her legs look like a stork's. And to make everything worse, the dress was way too big on top. It clasped behind her neck, halter-style, and gapped when she bent over a tiny bit.

And no bra would work underneath it. Every one she tried showed the strap, because the top of the dress angled up and in.

"Grace!" her mother called from downstairs. "You have to hurry!"

In exasperation Grace grabbed her one-piece bathing suit out of her drawer. It had a T-back kind of strap. Maybe it wouldn't show under the dress. Of course, once she put the dress on over it, that meant she wouldn't be able to go to the bathroom for the rest of the evening. She peeled off the dress, rolled it up, and stuffed it into her bag along with the bathing suit. Then she threw her wedge sandals on top. *Christina is right*, Grace thought grimly as she yanked on a shirt and shorts. The sandals were not only old and scuffed, but they would make her tower over most of the boys. She really was a walking fashion don't. With a sigh, she hurried out of her room and down the stairs.

"My, what a lovely house," said Grace's mother as they pulled into Jaci's front driveway. It was twice as big as the

Davises' house. Grace glimpsed the silver car in the garage, alongside an even fancier-looking one, and what looked like a swimming pool in the back. It amazed her to think Jaci would belong to RSC and also have her own pool.

Jaci's mom greeted her warmly at the door, waved to her mom as she drove out of the driveway, and sent Grace upstairs to Jaci's room.

As Grace headed up the deeply carpeted, wide stairway, she glanced to the right and the left at the downstairs rooms. It looked like a fancy house from a movie. Nothing was out of place, no shoes were in the front hall, no jackets had been flung on the backs of the couches. The furniture was funky and modern-looking, the colors all muted beiges and browns.

"Be right out!" called Jaci's muffled voice from inside her closet when Grace walked in. Grace had a little time to look around Jaci's room. It looked like one of those rooms you see in a decorating magazine, the kind of magazine Grace looked at only when she was in a doctor's waiting room and there was nothing better to read. The walls were a deep rose color, the bedspread a sophisticated pattern of huge orange and rose-colored blossoms, and the bed was strewn with about seventeen throw pillows in various shades of orange, rose, and a cool aqua blue. Grace wondered if Jaci made her bed every morning. *It must take about ten minutes to arrange all those pillows just so,* she thought. *Maybe they have a full-time maid who does it.*

At least the room looked like someone actually lived in it. The bookcase was full of books going every which way, and the large, L-shaped desk, built into one whole corner near the window, was strewn with papers, notebooks, and a sleek silver laptop. On one corner of the desk stood an actual microscope. Leaning up next to the desk was a black musical instrument case, which Grace realized must be Jaci's clarinet. Next to the music case was a music stand. Complicated sheet music was propped open on it.

Jaci stepped out of her closet and grinned at Grace. Her hair had come out of her ponytail and her glasses were slightly awry. Her arms were full of dresses on hangers. She staggered over to the bed and dumped the pile on top of it. "Just in time," she said, panting a little. "You can help me choose a dress to wear."

Grace's eyes widened at the sight of the pile on the bed. *There have to be half a dozen fancy dresses,* she thought in amazement. Some of them still had the tags on.

Jaci saw Grace's expression and shrugged. "When you're the only girl in a family with three brothers, and you have a mom who's way into fashion, she buys you a lot of clothes," she said. "I think it breaks my mom's heart that I just don't care about fashion very much."

Grace nodded to indicate that she felt the same way, but secretly she couldn't believe how lucky Jaci was. It must be so amazing to have such a pretty mother who was also nice and willing to buy you anything you wanted!

"So you want to get dressed?" asked Jaci, sorting indifferently through the dresses on her bed. "Which one should I try?"

Grace teased a dress out of the pile. It was pale blue and had a tulle skirt, like a ballerina's tutu. "This one is pretty awesome," she said. "Why don't you try this?"

"I don't want to wear sleeveless," said Jaci. "I bet they'll have the AC blasting, and I'm always freezing."

Grace picked up a red dress with fluttery sleeves. "This one?"

Jaci scrutinized it. "Yeah, maybe. I'll try it. Why don't you try on the blue one? I bet it would look good on you." She said it so casually, like it was no big deal. "I bet we're the exact same size."

Grace dropped her bag and stared at Jaci. "Are you sure? Don't you care if someone sees me in one of your dresses? What if you wanted to wear it somewhere else or something?"

Jaci snorted and casually peeled off her shirt and then her shorts. Grace wished she could feel as unselfconscious as Jaci seemed to, standing there in her bra and underwear. Grace watched Jaci step into the red dress, then put her arms through the sleeves and shimmy it up. "Let's just say I don't get out much, and I prefer it that way. Just help me zip this up the back, and then try that one on and see how it looks."

For the next half hour Jaci tried on dresses. Grace finally convinced Jaci to wear a deep pink, shimmery dress with capped sleeves and a row of tiny sparkly beads around the neckline. When Jaci pulled her hair out of her ponytail and shook it out around her shoulders, she looked almost glamorous. Grace couldn't decide among four dresses, each one of which fit her like a dream, but finally they both agreed that the pale-blue dress was the best. It fit snugly in the bodice and then floated away from her body at the waist.

"You look just like you're about to dance *Swan Lake*," said Jaci. "I mean that in a good way, of course."

Grace did a little twirl in front of the mirror, and the skirt obligingly swirled around her in a wide circle. She stared at herself in the mirror. She really did look amazing.

"Try these on," said Jaci, emerging from her closet with a pair of silver strappy sandals. They had a slight heel, but it was thick enough that she wouldn't wobble when she walked—and they were considerably lower than the wedges. They fit perfectly.

Jaci's mom knocked at the door and they ushered her in. She looked at both girls side by side and clasped her hands together. "Gorgeous!" she said. "Need any help with your hair or anything?"

Jaci grinned at Grace. "My mom is dying to give me a makeover. I'll wear some makeup if you do."

Grace grinned back. "Okay," she said.

One at a time, Jaci's mom sat the girls down on a swively stool in front of her bathroom mirror and applied makeup from a dizzying array of products on the counter. Pots, tubes, brushes, lipsticks, creams—Grace couldn't believe she had so many different products on her face, and yet when Mrs. Clifford was finished, Grace didn't look cakey or clownlike. She looked like a movie star ready for the red carpet. Her skin glowed with a silvery luminescence; her lips had just the faintest whisper of a pale-pink shimmer; her brown eyes looked twice as big as normal, expertly rimmed with subtle, smokey grays and browns. As a finishing touch, Mrs. Clifford parted Grace's hair on one side, then brushed it back and fastened a sparkly comb in it.

Even Jaci allowed herself to be painted and powdered.

She took off her glasses and put in some contacts. Grace had never seen Jaci without her glasses—even at the swimming pool.

When Jaci's mom was finished, she stepped back to survey her handiwork. Grace stood beside her and looked at Jaci, too.

"Wow," said Grace. "I never even knew you had those huge green eyes before. Now they're the first thing you notice on your whole face."

Jaci seemed pleased. Jaci's mom seemed thrilled. Then she looked at her watch. "Almost time to go," she said. "I'll grab my purse."

When she had gone, the girls stared at each other and giggled.

"All right, here goes nothing," said Jaci, scuffing off toward the stairs in her black patent-leather pumps. Grace did a little twirl to flare her skirt and then followed Jaci down the stairs.

Chapter Twelve

*I*t wasn't until they'd clicked themselves into their seat belts and were driving away toward the dance that Grace's euphoric mood started to change to a gnawing anxiety. She was heading to the dance, a place full of kids who were mad at her. What if people ignored her or, worse, were actively mean to her? What if she just stood in a dark corner all night and didn't get asked to dance once?

Maybe Christina and Max had spread the word to the entire middle school that she was to be shunned as an outcast. She'd heard that had happened to an eighth-grade girl named Meagan the year before. Everyone believed, rightly or wrongly, that Meagan had leaked information to the assistant principal about a plan by some eighth graders to skip school at the very end of the school year. The kids had gotten in trouble, and as a result, practically everyone ignored Meagan until the next school year started. Grace tried to imagine what that would be like.

At least Mel was speaking to her, although Mel would be away all summer. And Jaci was nice, even if she wasn't best-friend material. Okay, so her idea of fun was working in a smelly pigeon lab all summer. Grace was just happy to have someone who was willing to hang out with her.

Jaci really did look pretty. The pink dress fit her perfectly; it was one of the ones that still had a tag on it, and Grace had peeked at it. The dress had cost $250 and hadn't even been marked down. And now that her hair was released from its drab ponytail and Jaci's mom had brushed and arranged it, Grace could see that it had a natural waviness to it that she had never noticed before.

"Have a great time, girls!" trilled Mrs. Clifford as she pulled up in front of the Grand Oak Villa, where the dinner-dance was being held.

Grace had been there once before, to Cameron's athletic awards banquet last year, when he was a senior in high school. It had a huge room full of tables and an area for dancing. Tonight it was all lit up and lots of kids were streaming in.

"Grace's dad will be here at ten to pick you up," Mrs. Clifford called through the open passenger-side window as she pulled away.

Jaci pretended not to hear her mom call to them, but Grace turned around to thank her.

Inside, the room was decorated with strands of sparkling white lights all around the walls. The tables were draped with purple tablecloths and festooned with all different-colored paper flowers. No one was dancing yet, although a DJ stood in one corner, and a popular song was playing at a booming decibel level.

Most of the girls were dressed in bright, jewel-colored dresses; a few were wobbling around on high heels, while others had already taken theirs off and were holding them in their hands. Most of the boys stood in one big clump, looking uncomfortable in their coats and ties. Most of them wore sneakers, Grace noted.

She looked around for Christina, then spotted her chatting with Ashley and Lindsay near the refreshment table. Christina looked lovely in a sophisticated black dress, her dark hair pulled into a sweeping updo and studded with what looked like pearls. Max stood not far away, talking with Marc LaRocque and Alex Hernandez. He looked up and locked eyes with Grace. His face darkened and he quickly looked away.

Maybe a flying saucer will suddenly crash through the ceiling and beam me up, Grace thought.

Grace saw Christina look her way. Christina's eyes widened. Then Grace felt Jaci poke her in the ribs. "I just remembered why I hate contact lenses," Jaci yelled in Grace's ear. "I'm going to the bathroom to fix it. Be right back. Want to come?"

Grace was about to follow Jaci when she saw Christina beckoning. "I'll be fine here," Grace said.

As Jaci headed off toward the bathroom, Grace took a shaky breath, then walked over to where Christina, Ashley, and Lindsay were standing. Were they going to tell her off in public?

"You look amazing," said Christina. "I thought you said you were going to wear Candace's old dress. That is so not an old dress."

Ashley and Lindsay were staring at her outfit outright, looks of sheer astonishment on their faces.

"Yeah, I know," said Grace. "I changed my mind." She wasn't about to tell them she'd borrowed it, least of all from Jaci.

"It's a great dress," acknowledged Christina. "It even makes *you* look sophisticated!"

Lindsay and Ashley tittered. Grace felt her face flush. "Thanks for that compliment," she said.

Christina's face clouded. "I didn't mean it that way. You've gotten so sensitive, Grace. No offense."

"No offense," Grace echoed dryly.

"I'll go get Max," said Christina to the other two girls. "We need to get a table." She looked directly at Grace, and Grace understood full well she was not invited to sit with them.

As Christina strode away, Ms. Holmes came rushing up to Grace, Ashley, and Lindsay. She put an arm around Grace, then the other around both Ashley and Lindsay, and gave the surprised girls a big hug.

"I am so proud of you three!" she gushed. "You did such a wonderful job on your Tibet presentation! We're going to hang the mandala in the cafeteria! You all get an A, and well deserved!" She released them from the embrace and went swirling away like an autumn leaf, back into the crowd.

"Wow. We got an A!" said Ashley. "I think that might be my first ever!"

"I know, right?" said Lindsay.

Grace thought about that and wondered if it was really true that Ashley had never gotten an A. She was clearly smart. Did she not work hard, or was she just saying she never got A's so she wouldn't get a reputation for being a brain?

"And by the way," said Ashley, turning to Grace, "Max got his project done too."

"Oh! That's great!" said Grace. "Did he miss his concert?"

Lindsay chortled. "You kidding? He went to the concert. His dad's secretary did most of the project for him."

"Well," said Grace after an awkward silence. "See you, I guess."

They both looked at Grace. "We couldn't have done it without you," Ashley said.

Grace smiled but kept her lips closed so her braces wouldn't show. "I know. No biggie," she said, and turned and walked away.

It felt good to know they approved of her. She could sort of understand, in a tiny way, Christina's need to be accepted by this bunch, even though she still thought Christina made it way too high a priority.

Jaci suddenly materialized at Grace's side. "What a scene in the bathroom! There were several sobbing girls who'd just been broken up with by their boyfriends. And several more angry girls who were about to break up with *their* boyfriends. I couldn't get out of there fast enough."

Grace grinned. "They're already putting out the food," she said. "Let's eat. I'm starving."

Some servers wearing black pants and white shirts were bustling around near the long row of tables and steamer trays, carrying big, silver oblong dishes with domed tops, and setting them into the trays. Kids were already starting to line up for the food. Grace watched as Christina, Ashley, and Lindsay raced over to stake out a table, setting their evening purses down and beckoning over Max, Alex, and Marc. There were two empty chairs at that table.

"Where should we sit?" Jaci demanded.

"I don't care," Grace said, still stung by Christina's obvious effort to exclude her from the popular table. *How about Siberia?* was what she thought to herself.

"Let's sit with those guys," said Jaci, pointing in a way-too-obvious way toward Kevin and Emily and Malik.

Jaci can be pretty clueless sometimes, Grace thought. What if she didn't want to sit with those guys? They'd seen Jaci point, so it would be really obvious if they didn't sit there. "Sure," said Grace, and they went over to put their stuff down.

Rashid suddenly appeared at the empty chair next to the one Grace was standing behind. He wore an oversize red-and-white polka-dot bow tie with a dark-blue jacket that had a distinct sheen to it; you could see it when he moved. He looked hilarious, and actually kind of cute, too. "This free?" he asked.

"Um, yes," said Grace. She smiled at him and didn't even bother to cover her braces with her hand. He was too short to be boyfriend material. But she felt comfortable with him. And at least he was speaking to her.

"Cool. Then save it for me." He put his hands on his hips and looked at her. Then he gave a low whistle. "You know what, Grace? You clean up *real* nice!"

Grace laughed and bobbed a little curtsy. She wished she could be as comfortable and confident as he always seemed to be. "Thanks, Rashid," she said. "You don't look like your usual terrible self, either."

He bowed low. "Come on, you guys," he said to the group at the table. "I'm so hungry my stomach is starting to digest itself. Let's get some grub!"

The rest of the evening was more fun than Grace would have dared hope. She danced almost every dance—

several times with Rashid, who didn't trip over her feet at all, a couple of times with Kevin and Malik, and the rest with no one in particular, but just in a big group of kids. She loved the way her dress swished when she moved and twirled like a flower when she spun. She didn't see much of Christina, who seemed to be sticking to one corner of the huge room. At one point, as she walked breathlessly off the dance floor to get a drink at the refreshment table, Veronica Massey approached her.

"I finally got sprung from photography duty!" she said. "Now I can actually do some dancing!" She looked Grace up and down. "You look really pretty tonight, Grace," she said simply.

"Thanks," mumbled Grace. She was so stunned she didn't have the presence of mind to tell Veronica how pretty *she* looked, although she really did look amazing. But then, she always looked amazing. Still, Grace mentally kicked herself for not making a reciprocal comment.

Grace's dad came to pick them up at closing time. He had on his baseball cap, but luckily it was dark, so people probably couldn't see him. She and Jaci prattled away about the evening the whole way home. As Jaci got out of the car, she thanked Grace's dad for the ride, then turned to Grace and said, "Thanks for agreeing to come with me tonight. I actually ended up having a really good time."

"Thank you for loaning me this amazing dress!" said Grace with a smile.

"So I have this clarinet recital tomorrow? At two? Any interest in coming? No pressure or anything. It's probably the last thing you want to do," said Jaci.

"I'd love to," said Grace. "It would be awesome to hear you play."

Jaci beamed. "Thanks," she said. Then she leaned in and whispered so Grace's father wouldn't overhear. "Hey, how's the RSC plan coming along?"

Grace sighed. "Still working on it," she whispered back.

After Jaci had gotten out of the car, Grace's dad turned around to talk to her. "Mrs. Barber came by today," he said. "She was very appreciative of how you took care of Boomer, especially when he was sick and you noticed."

"Aw, it was okay," said Grace.

"She dropped off your payment," he continued. "And she gave you an extra fifty dollars for going beyond the call of duty."

Grace's jaw dropped. An extra fifty dollars! That

canceled out the fifty she'd given back to Max.

She did another calculation just before bed:

$37 savings
$64 Boomer
$25 Orbens

_____

$126
plus Boomer bonus: $50

_____

$176

plus $25 more from Orbens tomorrow night?
$201???

As Grace fell asleep that night, she thought about the summer ahead. Maybe it wouldn't be so bad after all.

Chapter Thirteen

Grace slept late Saturday morning. When she awoke, the sun was streaming through the curtains that she'd forgotten to pull closed the night before. It felt good to lounge in bed and not feel pressure to hurry and walk Boomer.

Boomer. The fifty-dollar bonus from the Barbers would make all the difference!

At Jaci's music recital, Grace sat with Jaci's mom and her equally elegantly dressed dad, as well as with Jaci's younger brothers. Jaci turned out to be really good; she was listed last in the program, and after Grace had suffered through a shrill flute, squeaky oboe, and some honky instrument she couldn't even name, played by a very small boy, it was a relief to hear Jaci's smooth, velvety clarinet. At the end she played a trio with a kid on the violin and another on the piano, and the audience gave them a standing ovation.

Grace babysat for the Orbens that night, and it was a much calmer evening than the previous Saturday. Robby was already bathed and rubbing his eyes sleepily, contentedly sucking on his weesie, when Grace arrived. After she put him to bed, she played board games with the older kids. They watched one DVD together, and then she read them a few books and they went right to sleep. She almost felt guilty when Mr. Orben came home later and handed her twenty-five dollars.

The second she got home that night, Grace went to her shoe box and pulled the money out. She added the twenty-five dollars to the pile of bills in the box. She counted and recounted—she had $201! Did she still feel like using the money to join RSC? she asked herself. Yes, she did. She wanted it more than ever.

The next morning her parents were just coming in from the grocery store, laden with bags, as Grace padded into the kitchen to toast herself a bagel. "I did it!" she said. "I earned the whole amount for RSC!"

Her mom and dad looked at each other, and then her mom set down her bags and came over and sat at the table with Grace. "We're really proud of how you set yourself that goal and worked to attain it," her mom said.

Grace looked from her mom to her dad, and narrowed her eyes. "Thanks. Is there a 'But—'?"

Her dad pulled a carton of eggs from a bag and put them down on the counter. Then he crossed his arms thoughtfully. "No 'but.' Not really, anyway. But"—he coughed—"your mom and I have talked about this a little, Grace, and while we agree that you have earned the right to join RSC, we're concerned that you will spend the whole summer socializing, and we want you to apply yourself."

The bagel popped up from the toaster, and Grace tossed it onto her plate before it burned her fingers. "Spend the summer socializing?" Grace echoed. "Dad. Mom. Summer is all *about* socializing and relaxing."

"Still," said her mom, "we're not entirely comfortable with the idea of you spending day in and day out there without any structure."

"You mean *your* structure," said Grace, slathering her bagel with cream cheese.

"Actually, no," said her mom. "Not just ours. Anyone's. Which is why we think it would be a very good thing for you to join the Riverside swim team."

"The *swim* team? I *stink* at swimming."

"You're very coordinated," said her dad. "You took years of swimming lessons and gymnastics. I've seen you and your brother do some pretty impressive acrobatics at Grandma's condo pool."

"That's *diving*, not swimming," said Grace. "And we were just messing around. I'm not like Cameron, Dad. I'm not the competitive type."

"It'll be good for you," said her dad.

Grace chewed a bite of bagel thoughtfully. Her immediate instinct was to disagree with her parents, just as a matter of principle. And yet, she was forced to admit that maybe joining the team wasn't such a terrible idea. It would give a little structure to her day. It would allow her to get to know a bunch of kids—wasn't Veronica on the team? It was a chance to start fresh, to belong to a cool, popular group of girls without Christina around. *In fact,* she thought with satisfaction, *Christina wouldn't be in the picture at all, for once.* And also—she caught her breath at the idea—Mike Morris was on the team. Maybe the boys' and girls' teams practiced at the same time.

"Okay," said Grace, standing up from the table and clearing her stuff.

Her mother's eyes went round with surprise. Even her father blinked at her unexpected acquiescence.

"Okay?" said her mother. "You mean, you agreed as easily as that?"

"Sometimes we middle schoolers surprise you," said Grace with a grin.

After breakfast, Grace galloped up the stairs to grab her money to give to her dad, so he could sign her up online right away. Then she called Jaci.

"I'm in," she said.

"You're officially joining? That's awesome!"

"I know. The only thing is, my parents are making me join the swim team."

"Oh," Jaci said. And then she added on, "'Kay."

"What's that supposed to mean?"

"Nothing. That's great. It's just a bunch of jocks, is all."

"That's fine," said Grace, more brightly than she actually felt. "I'm used to jocks. My brother is one. And if that's what it takes for me to belong to RSC, then I'm up for it."

After she and Jaci hung up, Grace lay back across her

bed and thought about the summer ahead. This would be her first summer without Christina playing a major role. She thought back to the previous summer, when they'd been so close. They'd hung out for hours, practically every day before Christina left for her camp. She thought back to when they were in kindergarten together, walking hand in hand out to recess, hanging side by side on the monkey bars. Grace's eyes misted up a little, but then she sat up. That was then. Now Christina had changed, and not for the better. If she, Grace, was going to have a fun summer, she had to take matters into her own hands and make sure she did. It was time to be her own person, out of Christina's shadow.

The last four days of school crawled by. Grace had no tests because all the teachers had had to file the grades the week before school ended. The eighth graders spent most of their days practicing for graduation. So classes were just busywork. In algebra they did math puzzles. In social studies they watched a movie about how the Egyptians built the pyramids and then another about Roman plumbing. In English they watched a movie of *Romeo and Juliet*. Grace secretly loved the Shakespeare movie, which took up three

English periods. She imagined herself in the role of Juliet, and Mike Morris as Romeo—minus the tragic ending with the bodies all piled up at the end, of course.

Thursday, the last day of the school year, was a half day. The teachers had all thrown in the towel by this point, so there were parties in practically all of Grace's classes. By the time the final bell rang, she was feeling queasy from all the soda, chips, and cookies she'd consumed.

Christina was already at her locker as Grace approached hers, carrying a large, heavy-duty garbage bag for all her junk. Christina smiled and rolled her eyes. Grace flinched, waiting for Christina's mean comment to descend. "Doing a little spring cleaning?" was what she said.

"Yep, you could say that," said Grace, feeling her jaw clench.

They were silent for a minute. Finally Grace spoke. "So, when do you leave for sleepaway camp?"

"Oh, ah, can't remember," said Christina vaguely.

That was odd. She usually knew the exact date and time she planned to leave.

"What about you? What are you up to this summer?" she asked Grace.

."Oh, just the usual random stuff," said Grace. She spun the combination, then opened her locker and began pulling junk out of it and stuffing it into the bag.

"Maybe we'll see each other around or something," said Christina, closing her locker and shifting her backpack onto her shoulder.

"Yeah, maybe. That sounds great," said Grace. She knew perfectly well Christina didn't mean it.

"Okay, well, bye."

"Yeah, bye."

Grace pretended to be busy inside her locker, but as soon as Christina had left, she stopped and watched her old friend make her way down the long hallway. Just a few stragglers were left, cleaning out their lockers. As she watched her go, Grace wondered if it was a sad walk. It was hard to tell from behind. No, she decided, Christina had obviously written her off and was done with her. Well, so be it. For once, Grace had backup. She was looking at a whole Christina-free, fun-filled summer at RSC. And she'd made a resolution not to be so shy around other people.

Friday morning, her first day of summer vacation, was also Grace's first swim practice. Had she made a huge mistake?

In the locker room she tried not to look at anyone as she quickly changed.

"Are you new here?" asked someone next to her just as she was shimmying into her suit. Quickly she pulled up the straps and turned.

"Yes, and I'm new at swimming, too," said Grace.

"I'm Lisa," said the girl. "It's a fun team. And don't worry. I stink at swimming. I like diving better."

"Me too!" said Grace. Had she said it too enthusiastically?

Lisa smiled. "You'll love Coach Dana. And Coach Michelle, the diving coach, too. She'll be here tomorrow."

Grace emerged from the locker room, relieved that her new red racer-back one-piece looked just like the style that most of the other girls were wearing. She hated the cap, which pulled at her hair as she tried to get it all shoved up and in. She noticed some of the other girls had tucked their goggles under the shoulder strap of their suits, so she did the same thing, but felt like a total copycat for doing it. They could probably all see through her; she was trying to pose as an experienced swimmer and they knew it. The last formal swim lessons she'd had were at day camp back when she was in elementary school, and those were at the lake.

The sun was still low in the sky, but it promised to be a warm day. Still, right now, at eight a.m., when even dog walkers should still be asleep, Grace shivered in the cool morning air. She'd never seen the pool when no one was in it. The surface of the water looked smooth and inviting, like a big vat of Jell-O. She wished she could jump in and have the pool all to herself, to dive deep down into the Blue World . . . . which actually looked gray in the dim light of early morning.

She looked for Veronica, but Veronica wasn't there. Hadn't she mentioned to Grace that she was on the team? She recognized a couple of girls from school but didn't know their names. Everyone else seemed to know one another, and girls were chatting away. Grace draped her towel over the bottom end of a chair and awkwardly sat down to wait, her arms clasped tightly around her middle from both nervousness and the chill in the air.

"Come over here with me. Let's stretch," said Lisa, who appeared suddenly next to Grace.

Grace stood up and followed her over to a spot on the pool deck, where they spread out their towels.

As they stretched, Grace noted that a girl called Jen seemed to be the undisputed leader. Laughing and chatting, she had that easy confidence and air of being the queen bee that Grace recognized right away. Maybe she was a star swimmer.

"Does the boys' team practice here too?" Grace asked Lisa, trying to sound as casual as she could.

"Yep. They're probably off running right now," said Lisa. "Coach Dana prefers to torture us in the water," she added with a laugh.

A couple of minutes later, Coach Dana walked out of the locker room and called them over. She was dressed in stretchy athletic pants and a pink sweatshirt, and her shiny blond hair was pulled back in a casual ponytail. She looked like a serious athlete—something about the confident swing of her shoulders when she walked, and how she seemed to be all muscle. She smiled at the group of girls huddled around her, and Grace decided it was a nice smile.

"Welcome to the RSC swim team!" she said. "I know most of you, but I do see a number of new faces. Let's make lanes one and two slower, three and four medium, and five and six fast. Split up into whatever lane you think you belong, and we'll start with a two hundred PSKS."

Grace's stomach clenched in panic. What was a PSKS? Lisa nudged her arm. "Don't worry. I'll show you what to do. It means pull, swim, kick, swim—eight laps each."

Grace nodded gratefully.

"After that," Coach Dana continued, "we'll do some ten-by-fifty drills so I can assess the new girls and see how much progress you veterans have made. All right? Everyone pick a lane and hop in."

Grace made a beeline for lane one. Several other girls did, too, including Lisa. They smiled at one another, as though they were all happy to bond with other slow-laners.

Halfway through practice, and Grace had already swum a zillion laps. Her goggles hurt her underneath her eyes. Her stomach felt empty and slightly nauseous, and her arms and legs ached. As she clung to the wall, panting after a two-lap breaststroke, she noticed a large group of boys traipsing along beside the pool deck. It was the boys' team, obviously, and they'd just gone for a strenuous run, from the looks of their red faces and sweaty hair. "Dry-land training," she heard one girl say to another. Grace was too exhausted to look for Mike Morris, and anyway, to him she was just one of a bunch of indistinguishable girls in swim caps.

By ten o'clock practice finally ended, and the pool was open to other members. Grace sat on her towel at the end of a lounge chair, too exhausted to stand up. Her ears were stopped up. Her fingers were crinkled like raisins. She couldn't remember the last time she'd felt so hungry. The boys' team had left the pool a little after the girls' team had, and she could see them sitting in a big clump around the coach near the boys' locker room, having a long chat. Some grown-up lap swimmers had appeared and were swimming placidly in their lanes. Exhausted as she was, the diving boards at the other pool beckoned to her. Just one dive, she told herself, and pushed her weary body off the chair.

It felt great to have taken off the swim cap, which hadn't even kept her hair dry. She stood at the end of the diving board and shook back her damp hair. Then she raised herself on her toes, took four quick steps to the end of the board, bounced, and dived into the pool.

Whoosh. Down, down into the comfortable, muffled world she loved so much. All too soon her head popped up and she pulled herself out of the pool with arms so weary and wobbly they could barely hold her as she pushed herself to a standing position and shook off the water like a wet dog.

"Wow! Nice!" called a voice behind her.

Grace turned. Coach Dana was addressing her.

"That was a beautiful dive, Grace," she said. "You look like a natural. Are you a gymnast?"

Grace swallowed. Speak up, she said to herself firmly. Don't stammer. "I was once. Not . . . not so much anymore. I got too tall," Grace said.

"Well, Coach Michelle will probably rope you in to her diving squad if you're not careful," Dana said with a smile. "She'll be at practice tomorrow."

Grace smiled a tiny smile and headed for her towel. Maybe joining this team wouldn't be such a disaster after all.

"Grace! Over here!" called another voice from across the pool.

Grace looked up. It was Lisa, waving her arms like she was landing an airplane. She had on shorts and a sweatshirt, her damp hair pulled back in a ponytail. Next to her were four smiling girls. "You want to go grab some food with us? Snack bar's open!" she called.

"Okay, sure!" said Grace happily. "I'll just throw something on and meet you there."

"Cool," said Lisa, and off they went.

Grace raced into the locker room and threw on her T-shirt and shorts over her suit, carefully rolling down her waistband as she'd noticed the other girls did. She remembered to stuff her wet towel into a plastic bag as her mother had begged her to do, then chucked it into her tote bag, along with her cap and goggles. Two minutes later, she was walking quickly—not running—along the pool deck toward the snack bar.

The warm sun was higher in the sky, glinting on the surface of the water. She liked the sounds of splashing, the smell of chlorine and sunblock, and the feeling of belonging to a team. *I've been invited to come eat with my teammates!* she thought happily, glad her mom had given her a few dollars for a snack before she left the house that morning.

As she approached the snack bar area, she skidded to a stop. There he was—Mike Morris! He was leaning against the counter, chatting with Jordan, the lifeguard, another teenage guy who worked behind the counter, and with a girl with long brown hair, whose back was to Grace. Just the sight of Mike made Grace's pulse quicken and her breath grow shallow. She could see his dimples from here!

He looked her way. He grinned and waved. Her knees buckled.

Suddenly the girl next to Mike turned around and Grace could see her profile. Grace gasped. It couldn't be.

It was.

Standing right next to Mike Morris was Christina Cooper.

Christina pushed a strand of hair behind her ear, and then her gaze rested on Grace. If she was surprised, she certainly didn't show it. She just smiled and waved. "Grace! Hi!" she called in her warmest Christina way.

Grace forced her feet to move. She made her way over to Christina. Mike, meanwhile, had taken his bagel and gone to sit down with some of his teammates.

The two girls stood a couple of feet apart and stared at each other. Christina smiled again. "Veronica told me she thought you might be joining RSC!" she said. "This is so awesome!" She peered at Grace's face. "You have, like, a big red line all around your eyes," she said.

"From my goggles," said Grace, trying to keep her voice from sounding as irritated as she felt.

"Oh! You're on the team? I had no idea you were any good at sports."

Grace let that go. "I thought you were going to your sleepaway camp," she said.

Christina shrugged. "Not this summer," she said. "That day at the mall? When you mentioned RSC? I thought, wow, wouldn't it be great to spend the summer at a swim club. And now, we can spend it together—just like old times!"

"Yeah, just like old times," Grace repeated dully.

Christina moved toward Grace and threw her arm around her shoulders. "It's going to be the best summer!"

"The best," said Grace.

"All right," said Christina. "I'm going to go find a prime spot to put my stuff. See you soon!"

"Bye," said Grace. As Christina walked away, Grace couldn't help but feel like each slap of Christina's flip-flops sounded like a slap in the face. Although she and Christina had kind of patched things up, their friendship was not what it once was. Grace had been so excited for a new start this summer.

She was jolted out of her thoughts by something hitting the back of her bathing suit. She looked down. It was a french fry.

"Hey, you!" said Lisa, a big grin on her face. "You joining us or what?"

"One sec," Grace replied. "Just trying to decide what to order."

Grace took a deep breath. She reminded herself that there were tons of new friends to be made at RSC. Maybe this summer would still be perfect. Maybe.

Ready for more?
Turn the page for an excerpt
from the second book in the
Pool Girls series,

Heat Wave!

Don't move."

Christina's eyes flew open. Standing right in front of her was Mike Morris. His broad, muscular frame blocked the sun, which made him look as though he were bathed on all sides by a glowing light. She could feel Lindsay and Ashley, who were lying on either side of her, stop breathing as Mike took a gentle step toward her.

Did he want to memorize the way she looked, lounging back on the chair in her new electric-blue bikini, her dark hair piled carelessly on top of her head?

With a quick whisk of the back of his hand across her forearm, he stepped back again and grinned. "Bee," he said.

"Be what?" asked Christina, giggling.

"I think it was a yellow jacket, actually," Mike continued, ignoring Christina's misunderstanding. "Crawling right on your arm. They love soda, so look before you take a sip. Those suckers really hurt when they sting, especially on your tongue."

She barely had time to stammer out a thanks when he turned and walked away. All three girls sat up and watched him walk to the other side of the pool, where the snack bar staff had just fired up the grill. He joined a group of swim-team guys who were scarfing down chips and dip.

"He is definitely superhot," said Ashley. "I can see why you wanted to join this swim club."

"Totally," agreed Lindsay.

"I wonder if he's part fish," mused Christina. "Maybe that's why he never notices me. He would rather be swimming in the dumb pool than anything else."

"Speaking of hot, it's hot," said Ashley, pulling her hair up into a flawless ponytail. "I'm all sweaty. But thanks for having us as your guests today! This looks like an awesome Fourth of July picnic!"

"Yeah, if your invite hadn't come through, I'd be spending the day at my aunt and uncle's house, listening to my aunt brag about how brilliant my cousins are," said Lindsay, rolling her eyes.

"I heard Marty at the snack bar say this was the hottest Fourth of July picnic he's ever organized. And he's been working here for forever," said Christina.

"Look, there's Veronica," muttered Lindsay. "Shocker. She's hanging out with the swim team. Again."

Christina's eyebrows went up. "I thought you guys were really good friends with Veronica."

"'Were' is right," Ashley said with a sniff. "She's become obsessed with the swim team. It's swim team this, practice that, Coach Dana blah-blah-blah. She never has time for doing important stuff with us."

Christina suppressed a smile. She hadn't been friends with Lindsay and Ashley for very long, but her impression was that they didn't actually do a lot of "important stuff," at least not that she'd observed. They seemed to spend most of their time shopping, texting, and surfing the Net. At least Veronica, who was also a member of this superpopular group, seemed to care about getting good grades. But Christina wasn't about to complain. This past school year her friendships with her old best friends, Grace Davis and Mel Levy, were totally strained. Grace and Mel just seemed a little immature. Christina was trying to help them grow up, but they didn't seem to like that. So Christina was happy to have these new friends and to be accepted as part of their group. "Yeah, Grace is totally all about the swim team," added Christina. "It's like it sucks you in."

"I'm going to dangle my legs in the water," said Ashley, swinging around and standing up.

"You're not going in?" asked Christina.

"No, I'm having too good a hair day to get it wet," said Ashley, tossing her glossy ponytail this way and that.

"I'll come too," said Lindsay, standing up and joining Ashley.

Behind her dark glasses, Christina sized up their bathing suits. Lindsay's two-piece was a really cool coral color, and Ashley's suit was lavender with pale-yellow polka dots. She darted a glance down at her own suit. Were bright colors out of fashion now? Was this so last summer?

"Coming?" asked Ashley.

"Nah, go ahead. I'm just going to lie here and think about how to get Mike Morris to notice me," said Christina, fanning herself with Lindsay's copy of *Teen Vogue* and looking across the pool at Mike over the top of her sunglasses.

"Okay, save us a seat if you go for food," said Lindsay, and the two headed off to the water.

A group of girls from the swim team walked up to the snack table. Christina saw her old friend Grace nudge Mike

Morris and say something. They both laughed. Christina gaped. How long had Grace and Mike been so chummy? And since when was Grace that comfortable around boys? She'd always been so painfully shy. Grace had barely spoken to her all summer. Was she mad that Christina had joined the club too? Christina sighed. She and Grace had known each other since preschool days. It was sad how people could change so much. Christina had tried so hard, both subtly and not so subtly, to help Grace grow up a bit, to add sophistication to her look. She had offered several times to take Grace under her fashion wing and consult with her about clothing and makeup. But Grace had been so sensitive about it. Christina eyed Grace's wet ponytail, casual T-shirt, and baggy shorts, and sighed. Hopeless. Grace might be enjoying her new popularity at RSC, but she still had no fashion sense.

"Hey! You hungry?" Christina heard a cheerful voice behind her.

Christina turned, saw who it was, and smiled. It was Jen Cho, her new-but-not-new friend. They had lived on the same block most of their lives, but they lost touch when Jen went off to Shipton Academy for middle school. But once they discovered they both belonged to RSC, their friendship blossomed again. And being friends with Jen definitely made Christina look good, especially around all those cliquey swim-team girls.

"I'm starved!" said Christina, grabbing her shorts. She pulled them on and stood up. The heat made her feel a little dizzy, and the air rippled above the hot pool deck.

"You shouldn't lie out in the sun like that," said Jen, shaking her head. "Not good for you."

"Yeah I know," Christina said with a shrug. "But it's too hot to do anything else, even swim!"

Jen laughed. "Well, now both the boys' and girls' swim teams are here, so you'd better get some food before they eat it all! Swimming makes us famished!"

"Hey, girls, can you give me a hand here?" called Coach Dana. She was standing next to three long metal tables that were folded up and propped against the snack-bar shack. "Marty thinks we'll need a few more tables set up. Here, Jen, help me carry this one over."

While Jen and Coach Dana carried off one of the tables, Christina looked around for another person to help her. And there was Mike, not five feet away.

"Hey, a little help?" she called to him.

He turned and trotted over. The two of them lifted the table. Christina admired Mike's arm muscles as he hoisted the other end of the table. He carried it so easily, as though it weighed nothing. "Thanks," said Christina as Mike set it up next to the one Dana and Jen had carried. She searched for something else to say. "So, hot enough for you? My mom told me that the weatherman says he has no idea when this heat wave will break."

"I don't mind the heat," said Mike. "Good excuse to go swimming again!" He gave her a melt-your-heart sideways grin, and loped away.

Christina sighed. Why, oh why, did he not seem the least bit interested in her? Did he have a girlfriend? Impossible. She'd have heard through the grapevine if he did. She crossed her arms and let out another sigh.

"Not worth it," someone whispered in her ear.

She whirled around to see Jen again, grinning this time. "What's not worth it?"

"Aw, come on. Any dope can see you're into him. Trust me: he's an okay guy and all, but the only thing Mike Morris cares about is swimming. And that's saying something, coming from me." Jen turned and followed after Coach Dana, who was waiting for help with the next table.

There's got to be some way to get his attention, Christina thought. Her gaze came to rest on Coach Dana, then traveled across the patio area to where the boys' coach, Paul, was standing, grilling hot dogs and waving away billowy smoke from the grill. "Hmm," Christina said quietly to herself. "I wonder if *he* has a girlfriend."

He was definitely cute, and just the right age for Coach Dana. Christina guessed that he was in college. He looked to be about the same age as Cameron, Grace's brother. Spiky brown hair; medium height; nice, muscular arms. The guys on the swim team all seemed to like him a lot. He struck Christina as a little intense about coaching, but then, so was Dana. Yes, Coach Dana could certainly do worse.

She turned toward Dana, drumming her fingers thoughtfully on her cheek. Definitely attractive, and maybe Paul's age or a year or two younger. *It would be nice if she paid a little more attention to her hair,* Christina thought, but that was a small detail that could be worked out.

This could be a project. A project for her and Mike!

Christina made her way over to Mike, who was talking to Coach Paul about split times, whatever those were, as Paul piled blackened hot dogs onto a plate. She sidled up to Mike and tapped him gently on the arm. "Pssst," she said. "I just had an idea. Got a second?"

Looking slightly baffled, Mike followed her over to one of the still-empty tables.

"What's up?" he asked as they sat down.

"I was thinking," she said slowly, taking a second or two for a dramatic pause, so his curiosity might grow. "I was thinking that Coach Paul and Coach Dana might make a good couple. What do you think?"

"Couple? Like, you think they're into each other?"

"Well, no, not yet," said Christina quickly. "That would be our job. To get them together. They both seem so obsessed with coaching and stuff, neither one seems to have noticed that they'd be perfect for each other!"

Mike scratched his head, still looking puzzled. "Why do you think they need to get together?"

Christina sighed. "Does he strike you as rather intense about swimming?"

Mike nodded. "Of course. Is that a bad thing?"

Christina nodded. "It's because he has no life outside of coaching. And neither does she. You can't live on swimming alone."

"You can't?"

"No. You can't. Once they realize they need each other, their lives will be complete. Don't you see? And anyway, it would be fun, like a summer project. For us. To do. . . ." She trailed off, then resolved to try again. "Do you know if Paul has a girlfriend?"

Mike shrugged. "Not sure. I *think* so, but we don't really talk about that stuff."

Boys could be so exasperating. How could he not know? Mike and Coach Paul spent hours together every day! "Well, find out, will you? Because if he doesn't, we can think of a way to get them together."

"Okay, sure," said Mike. "Good luck with that. Right now I smell cheeseburgers, and they're calling my name." He winked, gave her another half smile, and headed toward the grill area.

Christina watched him go. That was the longest conversation they'd ever had. Even if he didn't seem to get it, she was not going to give up on this scheme. She knew nothing about swimming, but she had excellent people skills. This matchmaking plan was almost too easy—the coaches were *perfect* for each other. And it would give her more reasons to talk to Mike. Once she got things up and running between the two coaches, Mike would have to see how cool it was to be in a relationship. It might turn his own thoughts to love . . . and she'd be there waiting for him when it finally dawned on him that she, Christina, was perfect for him.

Growing up, *Cassie Waters* spent every waking moment of every summer at her swim club (which was conveniently located at the end of her street). These days Cassie lives in the suburbs of New Jersey, writing and editing books, hanging out with friends, and having lots of fun. Over the years, Cassie has written dozens of books, but the Pool Girls series is nearest and dearest to her heart. She doesn't make it to the pool nearly as often as she would like these days, but she is still very good friends with the girls she used to hang out with at her swim club.